What the critics ~~

Cricket Starr

Fangs for the Memories

HOLLYWOOD AFTER DARK

ELLORA'S CAVE
ROMANTICA PUBLISHING

An Ellora's Cave Romantica Publication

www.ellorascave.com

FANGS FOR THE MEMORIES

ISBN #1419953745
ALL RIGHTS RESERVED.
FANGS FOR THE MEMORIES Copyright© 2005 Cricket Starr
Edited by Ann Leveille
Cover art by Niki Browning

Electronic book Publication August 2005
Trade paperback Publication February 2006

Warning:

The following material contains graphic sexual content meant for mature readers. *Fangs for the Memories* has been rated S-ensuous by a minimum of three independent reviewers.

Ellora's Cave Publishing offers three levels of Romantica™ reading entertainment: S (S-ensuous), E (E-rotic), and X (X-treme).

S-*ensuous* love scenes are explicit and leave nothing to the imagination.

E-*rotic* love scenes are explicit, leave nothing to the imagination, and are high in volume per the overall word count. In addition, some E-rated titles might contain fantasy material that some readers find objectionable, such as bondage, submission, same sex encounters, forced seductions, and so forth. E-rated titles are the most graphic titles we carry; it is common, for instance, for an author to use words such as "fucking", "cock", "pussy", and such within their work of literature.

X-*treme* titles differ from E-rated titles only in plot premise and storyline execution. Unlike E-rated titles, stories designated with the letter X tend to contain controversial subject matter not for the faint of heart.

About the Author

Cricket Starr lives in the San Francisco Bay area with her husband of more years than she chooses to count. She loves fantasies, particularly sexual fantasies, and sees her writing as an opportunity to test boundaries. Her driving ambition is to have more fun than anyone should or could have. While published in other venues under her own name, she's found a home for her erotica writing here at Ellora's Cave.

Cricket welcomes mail from readers. You can write to her c/o Ellora's Cave Publishing at 1056 Home Ave., Akron, OH 44310.

Also by Cricket Starr

Divine Interventions 1: Violet Among the Roses

Divine Interventions 2: Echo In the Hall

Divine Interventions 3: Nemesis of the Garden

Ellora's Cavemen: Legendary Tails 1 (*Anthology*)

Fangs for the Memories

Ghosts of Christmas Past

Holiday Reflections

Memories To Come

The Doll

Two Men and a Lady (*Anthology*)

Also check out Cricket's release **All Night Inn** *under her pen name Janet Miller at Cerridwen Press*
(www.cerridwenpress.com)

Fangs for the Memories

&

Chapter One

ಸಿ

Cleopatra drifted through the room like a dream—quiet, satisfying and unlikely to be remembered long. From his seat at the bar Michael watched and wondered. In the middle of a noisy West Hollywood nightclub she seemed to invite invisibility and it was the last thing you'd expect a movie star to do.

But then again, Cleopatra Lutz wasn't just any movie star.

With ever growing excitement he noted the way she examined the patrons out of the corners of her eyes without looking at anyone directly. She was trying hard to be unnoticeable. She pretended to sip her drink—straight up vodka, he'd heard her order it. He knew she could drink it if she needed to but since the volume in the glass never changed, the drink must be intended as protective coloration and not a beverage. Apparently Cleopatra wanted to keep a clear head.

Wise of her. Michael added that to the growing list of things he liked about her, that she knew when not to let alcohol affect her judgment. He chuckled into his glass as he took a small sip of his own beer before putting it down on the counter. He didn't need to be impaired either.

Given all the trouble she was going to, she'd probably be disappointed that he was aware of her presence. She apparently wanted to be invisible and in the midst of a club, with its noisy patrons, darkness, flashing lights and pulsating music, she probably felt she should be.

But Michael knew something about the slender dark-haired beauty the rest of the crowd didn't and that made it easy for him to spot her. It wasn't just that she was the late-night hostess of his favorite horror movie program. After all she did that in a lot of makeup and under a pseudonym, and he doubted anyone would recognize her from that. And it was more than her exotic looks that made her stand out, although those didn't make him want her any less.

The reason he noticed her was that now that he'd seen her in person and could feel the outer edges of her mind, he knew something that he'd only suspected before. From her mind he picked out what she was and her purpose in coming here tonight.

Michael grinned a little to himself. He knew why her eyes tracked the young men in the club like a cat in heat would watch a tom, her body on fire for the body of a compatible male.

But unlike the cat, it wasn't just sex she craved. Cleopatra was out for blood—literally.

He'd heard the rumors but now he knew for certain. The lady was a nightwalker, a vampire who needed the blood of others to sustain her life. Any sex she got tonight would just be a bonus for her and her happy "victim".

For a moment Michael savored how fortunate he was. What were the chances that he'd spot her when she was hunting and he was unbound? It was rare he even came to a club like this. He could almost believe divine intervention was involved in leading him here to find her.

Nearly unconsciously his fingers stroked his neck to feel the smooth, unblemished skin. He missed the roughness of the pinpoint marks that had once designated him Vladimir Rostin's sworn companion.

When a nightwalker took a companion, they left the marks of their first feeding, the twin scars from their fangs containing small amounts of vampire DNA. The marks allowed the companion's body to change, to make more blood than an ordinary human, rich blood that sustained a nightwalker best and kept them healthy. A nightwalker might feed several times a week from his or her companion—but it was more than a bargain. In exchange the companion enjoyed the nightwalker's protection, plus better health and a slower aging process.

Michael had been Vladimir's companion for many, many years, but that had come to an end a few months ago when the nightwalker had met Samantha, an art student at UCLA. It hadn't been a surprise when Vlad brought the pretty co-ed home after she'd turned up in the nightwalker professor's evening art history class. What kind of former nobleman nightwalker could resist choosing a blonde California valley girl as a regular blood donor? But then it had turned out that Sam was Vlad's bloodmate, the only source of nutrition he needed—a relationship far more intense than a simple companion.

It had been obvious from the beginning that eventually Vlad would have to release him and remove the scars on his neck. He didn't blame his former master. Bloodmate companions were extremely rare and highly valued. A bloodmate and nightwalker were nearly always sexual partners, their minds as intimate as their bodies, and the closest thing to a spouse a nightwalker could have.

Once Vlad had Sam in his life, Michael had to go. A nightwalker might keep several companions, but only one bloodmate, ever.

Bloodmate. Even now, the title caused a pang. Michael might not resent Sam but he couldn't help envying her position with Vlad. Becoming a bloodmate was something all companions spoke about with longing, but few achieved.

Michael shook his head to clear it of wistful thoughts and resumed his observations of Cleopatra. He didn't know what her situation was but since she was hunting, it was likely she didn't have enough companions to keep her fed. If she liked him he might have a chance of getting a position with her.

A position with Cleopatra Lutz, legendary movie star...even if only as a companion, he couldn't ask for anything better. He'd harbored a fondness for her ever since he saw her in one of her earliest films when he was a boy.

Okay, more than a fondness. By the time he was sixteen she populated even his most intimate dreams and the first time he'd jerked off it had been with her image in his mind. He'd been devastated when she'd disappeared without explanation from the movies, but intrigued when years later he'd heard rumors that she might have been converted into a nightwalker. The only problem had been locating her.

Obviously she was something of a recluse. The other parafolk had no idea she was around. When her alter ego "Deloris DeNight" had shown up on television on the *Bloody Night* television show, he'd wondered if it had been Cleopatra under all that makeup but couldn't prove anything.

It really was a stroke of luck finding her tonight. He'd thought to visit one of the regular parafolk hangouts to see if he couldn't find another nightwalker to companion, but this was a lot better. For one thing, she was a female nightwalker and those were actually rather rare. You could only become a nightwalker by drinking the blood of another nightwalker, and most male nightwalkers would rather keep their ladies companions rather than create another mouth to feed. Why create competition when you could have a devoted blood source instead?

Across the room Cleopatra continued perusing the crowd, her attitude screaming impatience. She was hungry, very hungry, unless he missed his guess. Michael smiled to himself. He'd take care of that soon enough.

It had only been a few days since Vlad had released him and even with the marks removed he was still close enough to being a companion to give her the best feeding of her life. She certainly could use one.

He wondered when Cleopatra had last enjoyed a good companion-feed. At least a while, he could tell. She didn't have the glow a nightwalker had when they fed regularly from a companion and she seemed almost sickly, like her diet consisted only of norms.

It also had been a while since she'd hunted in such a public place. Michael could tell that by the way she was dressed and how out of place she seemed. The club was filled with the young and trendy, wild clothes and wilder hair, with visible piercings galore.

By comparison, Cleopatra was smooth elegance, her long black hair curling down her back like a waterfall of night against the shocking white of her skin, bared by her low-cut midnight-blue cocktail dress. Michael watched her shocked glances at the shorts, miniskirts and bared, pierced midriffs of the other women in the club, and swallowed a smile. She really hadn't gotten out much if she'd thought her outfit appropriate for a modern nightclub.

Her garment would have been most appropriate at one of the paranormal clubs he liked to frequent. For a moment Michael wondered why he hadn't seen her at one of those places. She'd have fit in beautifully there and would have had no trouble finding a suitable blood donor to feed her, with no need for subterfuge. Many norms loved going to the paranormal bars just for that purpose.

Here she was most definitely out of place. Still, she tried to keep it under control, tried to manage her need for nourishment as well as her visibility to the crowd. From her loose thoughts Michael picked up that she wanted to find someone and get him alone as quietly as possible.

She hunted for a single male — young, healthy and alone. Someone who wouldn't be missed for a while. Intoxicated or otherwise impaired, but not too much so. Michael took another sip of his beer to make himself more attractive. He doubted she wanted too many toxins mixed with her dinner, but she did need her dinner's judgment impaired enough to come with her without too much comment. It was important to her to remain invisible to everyone else — otherwise she might blow her cover and make it obvious what she was.

For himself, Michael watched her work with secret amusement. After all, he'd made up his mind as to just whom it was Cleopatra Lutz was going home with tonight. She was going home with him. She just didn't know it yet.

For an instant Cleopatra froze in the middle of the crowd and turned slowly in a circle. Michael sensed the path of her mental probe long before it reached him.

Crap, she must have heard that last thought of his. He hadn't thought he was broadcasting, at least not loud enough for her. Nursing his beer, Michael moved a little to one side and made his mind as innocent as possible.

Her gaze fixed on him, and he could feel her sudden mental attention. Oops, bad idea. No one thought innocent thoughts in a place like this. Michael picked a nearby woman with golden hair and ogled her deep cleavage, letting thoughts of letting his tongue slip between her breasts fill his mind.

It wasn't that hard to imagine. The blonde really did have nice tits. Even so it was Cleopatra's pale exotic face he allowed to superimpose itself over the woman's fair features in the most hidden part of his mind.

Cleopatra's mental probe disappeared immediately.

So, something of a prude. Tearing his gaze away from the other woman's bosom, Michael had to struggle not to laugh out loud. He didn't want to draw attention to himself, at least not quite yet. This was too much fun, watching her, imagining what he was going to do with her when he got her alone, all that lovely nightwalker beauty his to touch. To caress, hold and feed.

Michael closed his eyes for a moment. To feed…oh yes. To give her everything she wanted, to be anything, everything she needed. Maybe even become her bloodmate. He hadn't considered that possibility in the past—with Vlad it would have been impossible and no other nightwalker, male or female, had ever appealed to him the way Cleopatra did. She might not want him that way, but a man could dream couldn't he?

He could almost feel the tender bite of her fangs in his neck as he imagined sliding into her. It was going to be glorious, marvelous, the experience of a lifetime. Part of him wanted to rush to her side, but it was still a little too soon. Better to wait until she was ready to make her move then enter the scene. He wanted to watch her hunt for a while longer before revealing just who was really hunting whom.

A man approached her, more than a little scruffy, his blond hair cropped so short it was little more than a pale fur against his head. The newcomer sidled up to her and slid a strong possessive hand around her upper arm and immediately Michael's amusement disappeared. Cleopatra pulled back from him, but the guy's grip grew tighter and he leaned over to whisper into her ear. Something dirty, Michael decided from the look of distaste on her face. She leaned back and glared into the blond's face, her annoyance palpable across the room. The blond just grinned nastily at her and tightened his hand, digging his fingers into her flesh.

Irritation demolished Michael's self-imposed *laissez-faire* attitude and he glared at the interloper.

Fun was fun, but no one was going to treat his nightwalker that way! Leaving his barely touched beer on the counter, Michael headed in for the rescue.

Well this was another fine mess she'd gotten herself into. Cleo glared up at the blond-headed vermin holding her arm and considered her options. Sinking her fangs into his throat and sucking his blood until his heart gave out—or at least until he let go of her? Tempting, but it just wasn't an appropriate choice in the middle of a crowded nightclub.

After all, she was trying to maintain a low profile, and making someone a corpse in the middle of a crowd would definitely blow her cover. Blood-sucking was out.

So what else could she do? She'd tried to make him go away with a mental push, only to strike an unnatural obstruction to controlling him. As far as she could tell he didn't have any mental powers so it wasn't any kind of natural block. She could read his nasty little mind—unfortunately—but she just couldn't make him do her will.

Leaning forward she sniffed then gagged. From the stench of his skin and breath, she suspected he'd taken some sort of drug that inhibited her ability to control him.

Just terrific. She would meet a druggie she couldn't master the one time this week she went out for dinner. Some nights it just didn't pay to get out of bed.

It was all the fault of this day and age. In the past the worst you encountered was alcohol, which only gave her a pleasant buzz, but recently the chemical cocktails norms imbibed had all sorts of side effects, including this one, of strengthening a normal person's resistance to mental manipulation. Good thing she'd already decided against feeding from him. No telling what the drugs he was on would do to her.

Cleo allowed herself a mental sigh. If she couldn't use mental persuasion, she'd have to use physical instead. Perhaps a well-jabbed finger into his side would be effective...assuming what he'd taken didn't kill pain the way it obviously did brain cells.

She was just considering where to hit him when she felt a reassuring presence come up behind her. It was someone big, male, and when she sniffed she detected a faint spicy scent. Opening her mind she felt a mental warmth so inviting she had to catch herself from leaning back into it.

Over her shoulder came a deep masculine growl and she saw her captor's eyes widen. His hand on her upper arm grew damp and his odor soured under the newcomer's implicit threat.

Blondie swallowed hard then seemed to find his lagging courage. "What...do you want?"

A rich voice sounded in her ear. "The lady promised me a dance. I'm here to claim it."

A dance? Cleo puzzled over that one. Did people still do that, promise dances? It sounded so old-fashioned. She certainly hadn't promised anyone a dance anytime in the past fifty years. The pretext was so archaic it made her smile.

Obviously the guy behind her was trying to rescue her from the creep whose slimy hands still clutched her. She just wished he had come up with another excuse.

Not that she didn't love dancing, but the music had changed from her time and she couldn't imagine trying to keep pace with the driving beat of sheer sound that currently held the room hostage. On the other hand, going through the motions of dancing with the guy behind her was likely to be a far more pleasant experience than being in this guy's clutches.

Cleo turned her head to check out the pleasant-smelling man behind her.

Oh, yes…much nicer. Cleo couldn't help but smile up into the deep brown eyes gazing down at her. Dark hair in a short modern cut surrounded a thin face with an amused smile, sitting on top of the broadest shoulders she could remember seeing. She took a quick scan of the rest of him. Well-constructed arm and chest muscles clad in a black T-shirt under a soft black leather jacket, and there was an impressive bulge at the front of his fashionably faded denim jeans. She almost purred her approval. Where had this guy been all her life?

Wait a minute. She leaned closer. She knew where he'd been…this was the guy she'd sensed looking down the woman's top, whose admiration had been so blatant that she'd turned away from his lustful thoughts. Then he'd been easy to read but now she felt a blank wall when she tried to scan his thoughts. Whoever he was, he had mental powers far in advance of what she was used to.

Still, it didn't matter. She could use a good rescue and for the present he would do nicely.

"I was wondering where you'd gotten to," she said, dropping her voice into a sultry purr.

She watched his amusement deepen into an appreciative grin of even white teeth. For not the first time Cleo regretted she couldn't give in to an equally broad smile. Having permanent fangs did pose one problem—having to hide them. Outside of Halloween, or her late-night television show where her pointed incisors were considered part of the makeup she always showed up in, she could never simply smile without making someone wonder why she had such odd-looking teeth.

Cleo tried to return his smile by keeping her lips drawn tight across her upper teeth. She held up her free hand. "So, shall we dance now?"

Her rescuer took her hand and turned a brown-eyed glare with the intensity of a laser blast onto the other man. Even out of the direct line of fire Cleo felt its heat.

"If you'll excuse us," he said, voice laden with menace.

Punk-guy seemed to be in a mood to argue, but her rescuer didn't give him a chance. With a move so fast and smooth Cleo almost didn't follow it, the newcomer's hand shot out to press a nerve in the punk's elbow and the hand on her arm suddenly went limp. She pulled away and allowed her hero to lead her through the crowd. She spared one quick pleased glance back at the bar to see Blondie cradling his arm, a shocked look on his face.

Served him right for grabbing her.

Her satisfaction faltered when they grew close to the writhing bodies that crowded the dance floor. Cleo pulled on his arm. "I'm not much of a dancer."

"Not to worry," he said, all confidence. "I'll do the leading. All you need to do is follow." He grinned down at her with those perfect teeth. "You can follow, can't you?"

Well, yes, of course she could. At one time Cleo had had the best dance training the movie studios could offer. She knew how to foxtrot, to waltz, and could do a mean tango, all the classic dances of her day. It wasn't her fault that her days were long over and that kind of dancing out of fashion. What she saw on the floor around her seemed to be a lot of barely clad bodies randomly jerking about. Add in the club's heavy darkness, flashing lights and music so loud that she could barely hear her own thoughts, and she couldn't say dancing appealed much to her at the moment.

Her rescuer didn't appear to have similar issues. Expertly he guided her through the crowd to an open space on the floor and tugged her into his arms, cinching her tight against him. "Now just relax and move with me," he told her, his voice a whisper in her ears. "Think about it just being the two of us moving together."

A shiver went up and down her spine at the dark promise in his voice, a thrill that kept time with the driving beat of the music. Somehow she knew he meant far more than dancing with his words. Her stomach growled, but that wasn't half as significant as the heat building up between her legs.

Hungry as she was, it had been even longer since she'd had sex.

They began to move, not with the beat but in slow counterpoint to it, Cleo's body following his lead as they danced around the floor. To Cleo's surprise it was far easier than she thought to keep up with him. They moved along the dance floor together in synchronized rhythm, moving slower than those around them but with the music. She relaxed in his arms and gloried at their strength around her.

For the first time in...what had it been, thirty years, maybe? However long it was, Cleo danced and enjoyed it thoroughly. Her feet glided along the floor and she felt as light as a feather, the way she felt when she flew in the sky beneath a full moon.

More than that, dancing with this glorious unknown male touched something else inside her. Awareness of him flowed in her, awareness of more than his blood and the potency of his body, although those would have been sufficient on their own.

There was also the presence of his mind near to hers but still evading her probe. He seemed to surround her with his strength, in his mind, and from the hardness of his body, particularly the hardness of that very intriguing bulge in his pants, which now slid suggestively against the juncture of her thighs.

Her senses woke to full erotic alert, heat building within her pussy as she imagined just how good something that big would feel driving deep within her. This was no weak-minded delivery boy she was with, easy to catch and easier to drink from.

This was a man and the capture promised to be as good as the chase! Her mind filled with thoughts of how she was going to get him away from the club. Did she dare take him to her home? She had that four-poster bed of hers which had seen as little action in the past few years as she had. This could be a great time to get some use out of it.

Cleo lowered her head to his shoulder and leaned in to get a good whiff of him. Oh, he smelled delicious, the most delectable male she'd smelled in ages. She couldn't help moving closer, and then his neck was next to her mouth, his scent intoxicating and drawing her closer.

His heartbeat pounded in her supersensitive ears, the pulsing artery just inches away. Unable to resist, she leaned over to taste him, letting the tip of her tongue slide along the thick rich vein in his neck.

Outwardly she held her moan, but inside she thrilled at his delicious taste. This was going to be great…the best feeding in a long time. She slid her tongue along his neck again, her mouth watering over his flavor. Just a little taste of him. That's all she wanted.

Not here, Cleopatra. We're too exposed.

Cleo jerked back at the voice in her head. "What?" she whispered aloud, staring up at the man she danced with.

He stared back, a smile playing across his face. *This isn't the time or place. I know you're hungry, but I can't feed you on an open dance floor.* He hugged her closer, rubbing her bare back with the flat of his hand, the gesture blatantly possessive.

Wait until I get you home, then you can have all the blood you want.

Fear dried Cleo's mouth, making it a desert. Oh, god, he knew what she was…even worse he knew her real name. He might have recognized her from the television show and guessed she really was what she pretended to be. But on *Bloody Night* she used a pseudonym and there was no reason for him to know that Deloris DeNight was actually former movie star Cleopatra Lutz, a ninety-nine-year-old vampire.

From her earliest days as a vampire she'd followed the rules her maker had laid down. Don't tell anyone what you are—don't even let them guess. When they did you ran, you hid or you killed, and killing was always a last choice. Who and what they were was a secret, just him and her for so long, feeding carefully, always quietly, always alone.

Rodriquez had taught her the best way to avoid notice, the way he'd lived for centuries, and there were no others she knew about in all of Los Angeles. At least she'd never encountered any others.

Not that she got out much, but even so, in seventy years you'd think she'd have run into at least one other like her. After Rodriquez had died, she'd assumed she was completely alone.

She'd been so careful to avoid notice—and this man knew anyway. How could he possibly have guessed the truth?

Perhaps he didn't know for certain. She tried to bluff him out. "I don't know what you mean," she said, as if he'd spoken aloud.

Deep amusement covered his face. *It's all right, Cleopatra. I'm okay. Safe. I'll never hurt you.*

Damn straight he wouldn't hurt her! She'd never let him get close enough. Cleopatra Lutz hadn't lived all these years as a vampire in the heart of Los Angeles by not knowing how to disappear when things got tough.

With a sudden movement she broke away from him, turned and ran, heading for the club's emergency exit. With any luck they were up to the fire code and the door would open easily.

As she made her way through the crowd, ignoring the muffled complaints of other patrons, Cleo berated herself for her stupidity. She'd known it was a mistake to come here tonight, to hunt in such an open environment. She would have been better off seeking sustenance among the homeless, even if their sometimes-tainted blood left her feeling ill.

Better sick than dead as Rodriquez had always said.

She made it to the side emergency exit and was relieved to find it unlocked and even better, unalarmed. Probably kept that way to allow the smokers a place to light up.

Opening the door, she ran into the alley beyond, startling a couple of people lighting up. She rushed past them and through their cloud of smoke and around a corner to encounter a couple doing…what?

In spite of her hurry, Cleo couldn't help slowing down and throwing a more than passing glance at the pair of lovers backed up against the wall, lips welded together, the guy's hand on the woman's breast, and one of her legs sliding up and down the back of his.

Just as Cleo came near, there was the sound of a zipper, and then he lifted the woman and thrust forward. Breaking her stride, Cleo stared at them. Pretty impressive that a norm could fuck a woman against a wall that way. The man pounded into her with surprising strength, all to the woman's happy cries. Her legs wrapped around his waist, and the muscles in the man's ass clenched as he drove into her again and again.

A brief moment of dismay swept through Cleo as she watched them. Too bad the man she'd met had turned out to be so dangerous. It had been a long time since she'd made love and she really could have used some up-against-the-wall action.

Her sigh must have been too loud. The woman opened her eyes and glared at Cleo, and reluctantly she moved further down the alley. Watching them would have been fun, but no point in incurring any more trouble tonight.

Coming to where the club stored its garbage cans, she wrinkled her nose at the smell and sped past them to where the air was sweeter. Finally she was alone in the alley, the coupling couple left far behind and only emptiness around her. It was a dark night, the stars impossible to see through the city lights, and even the crescent moon was hard to make out through the haze.

If it had been full she would have been able to fly up into the air and away, but for now all she had were her feet to provide escape. She needed to run and hide from the man who knew her secret.

Fear made her speed up again. Run fast. Very, very fast. Too bad she was wearing heels instead of her running shoes.

Finally she reached the end of the alley where it met the street. From behind she heard no pursuit...maybe she'd lost him. Confidence growing, Cleo headed for the sidewalk and freedom.

But then two dark shapes detached from the dark shadow of the walls near the exit and then the glare of a flashlight shone into her eyes. Cleo gasped with open mouth and hugged the wall behind her. Realizing what she'd done, her hand flew up to cover her mouth but it was too late.

"So," a coarse voice spoke, tone sinister. "I see the rumors about you are true, Ms. DeNight. You are an undead creature of the night."

Cleo smothered a groan. How many years had she gone unobserved and now she'd been spotted twice in one night? This had to be a record of some kind. Served her right for going out to dinner rather than ordering in. Usually she called for some variety of home delivery food and tipped handsomely in exchange for a moment of the delivery person's time…well, their time and a little blood. Not enough to hurt them and she always clouded their minds so they remembered nothing.

Trouble was that the last pizza delivery boy she'd had for dinner had been high as a kite and it had taken two days for her to recover. She'd been leery of takeout ever since.

Something shiny appeared in one of her attacker's hands, and Cleo tensed, expecting a knife. To her relief it turned out to be a large metal crucifix, which he brandished with extreme menace in her direction. She looked at it and almost laughed. It wasn't even silver.

Well, they might have identified her, but obviously they didn't know a lot about vampires. Resisting the urge to roll her eyes, Cleo took a step forward only to see her cross-wielding foe pull a small vial from his pocket and throw it in her direction. Water splashed across her face, momentarily blinding her until she wiped it away with the back of her hand. She glared at the dampness, her amusement plummeting as she realized her dress had gotten splattered as well.

Dang it, she'd just had this dress dry-cleaned. Thoroughly irritated, Cleo stepped forward and grabbed the cross from her opponent's hand. She held it up in front of his astonished face. "Does it look like I'm afraid of this? I don't know where you get your nutty ideas, but whatever you believe about me, you are wrong. I'm not an undead anything."

"But the teeth," one of them stuttered.

"These?" she spoke crossly, pointing to her fangs. "Since you know my name, I assume you know I occasionally host *Bloody Night*, a late-night vampire TV show. These are part of my costume." She reached up and pretended to tug on one. "I accidentally used the wrong glue on my fangs a couple nights ago and wasn't able to get them off. I need to see a dentist about it."

She wasn't sure if she was convincing them, but at least at the moment they didn't look like they were going to drive a stake through her heart. Since she'd passed their first tests some doubt was seeping into their tiny minds.

Cleo breathed a short sigh of relief. She might be able to get out of this without a fight. "Now, if you gentlemen will excuse me, I've had a tiresome evening and just want to go home."

They still looked uncertain, but then the one with the flashlight shrugged his shoulders and gestured that she could leave. With profound relief Cleo handed the other his cross and started to push past them but then startled when she heard the familiar voice of her rescuer from the bar behind her.

That was odd…she hadn't heard his approach. The man moved as quietly as she did when she wanted to.

"Well, well, well…whatever is the Paranormal Watchers Society doing hanging out in the alleyway of a nightclub?" he said in a slow drawl. "Isn't this slumming for the likes of you?"

The eyes of both men narrowed. "Mr. Brown, how interesting to find you here." The flashlight holder lashed out to grab her arm and examined her more closely in the blinding beam. "Perhaps she isn't as innocent as we thought. Not if she's in the company of a known vampire companion."

Vampire companion…what the heck was that? Curiosity warred with Cleo's innate sense of survival.

Brown raised his head and glared at the pair. "You will unhand the lady now, or I'll make you wish you were both dead."

"As dead as you are?" the cross-holder taunted, "or as dead as she soon will be." Instead of the crucifix, a gun appeared in his hand, pointing right at her heart. "I'm armed with silver bullets."

Cleo couldn't help her shudder as true fear swept over her. Silver was one of the few things she did have trouble tolerating—that and sunshine. A silver cross would burn her and she wasn't able to break silver chains. Even if he missed her heart, a silver bullet could still kill her if it was left in her long enough.

She really should not have gone out tonight. Just because she'd had a mad desire for something fresh...something tasty, less fatty and healthier than a pizza delivery boy. How terribly inconvenient. All these years of living safely, living peacefully, and she was going to die just because she had gone out for a more nutritious dinner.

A heartfelt sigh escaped her. It just really wasn't fair.

Chapter Two

𝔰𝔬

The man the others called Brown moved quicker than Cleo thought a normal human could possibly move, grabbing for the gun with a lightning-fast hand. Even so as he seized it, it discharged, and she felt the bite of a bullet through her upper arm. It tore through her with a burning sensation that told her the man had been telling the truth about the silver metal in his bullets. Cleo cried out at the pain.

When he saw she'd been hit, Brown's face fixed in fury and he grabbed both men by the scruff of their necks, slamming their heads together with a sound not unlike that of two melons colliding. He released them and the pair slid to the ground to lie in a broken heap in the alley. Only their continued breathing told Cleo they were unconscious rather than dead.

Brown must have noticed her worried look and he shook his head. "I don't kill if I don't have to." He took in how she was holding her upper arm and pulled her hand away to examine the wound in the pale light. His eyes narrowed and mouth set in a thin line as he collected the fallen gun. "It isn't too bad. The bullet passed right through the muscle. You won't need a doctor, not once you've fed."

"It was silver," she whispered. "There will still be some in the wound."

He nodded. "Yes, but I can deal with that." Some of his good humor returned. "This is the second time I've rescued you tonight, Cleopatra Lutz. I think you better come home with me for safekeeping." Brown grabbed her by her uninjured arm and directed her to a nearby parking lot. "I can see I'm going to have my work cut out with you."

She rallied her self-composure. "I was going to get by them before you showed up. I had them convinced I was an actress."

"You are an actress, Cleopatra. One of the best. But even so, you shouldn't be out alone like this, not with the PWS running loose." He led her to a sleek dark-colored car and placed her into the passenger side before getting into the driver's seat. She waited for him to start the car, but he watched her instead. Then he reached around her to grab a belt from the side of the car and buckled it across her.

Cleo felt faint as his warm large body covered her for just that small moment of time.

"Don't you believe in safety?" he asked when he had her secure.

"Well, of course I do," she said, but said nothing more. How was she going to explain that the last time she'd ridden in a private car had been so long ago that safety belts hadn't even been invented, and she didn't use them in the rare cab rides she took. She always took the bus to the studio for her nighttime tapings, just as she'd done to the nightclub tonight.

Brown shook his head disapprovingly and started the car and pulled out into traffic. He drove down the road towards the ocean. To his home he'd said, and Cleo wondered for a moment where he lived.

The motor hummed with a powerful sound, a neat purr that Cleo could have leaned into, just as she had leaned into Brown earlier when they'd danced. In the confined space of the vehicle, his heady scent tickled her nose and her hunger woke, for more than just his blood. Between her legs her sex awakened, teasing her awareness of him. His scent changed, became earthier, and she knew he was aware of her as well.

"Cleopatra…"

"Please, call me Cleo," she said.

He glanced over at her and smiled. "Cleo then. And you should call me Michael."

"Michael. Michael Brown?"

"The one and only."

It was a nice name she decided. Comfortable and solid, not unlike the man himself. But her arm ached, growing worse by the minute as the silver seeped into her bloodstream. The car hit a bump the suspension couldn't adjust for and she let out a low moan as she was jostled against the seat.

Michael gave her a longer look and immediately slowed the car, pulling into a convenient parking lot.

"What is it, Cleo?" he asked, quiet concern in his tone. "Does your arm bother you?"

"It hurts," she admitted through clenched teeth.

He passed his hand along her face and down her arm, as if using some innate sense to read the state of her body. A worried look crossed his face. "You've lost blood, and the silver is working faster than I'd expected. Plus you haven't been eating properly for a while." He frowned. "I was going to wait until we got to my place, but I don't think we can."

With a swift movement he rolled up his shirtsleeve and bared his wrist. He held it under her nose, offering it to her. "I'll control the feeding, but you need to drink at least a little now."

It was too easy. Cleo stared at him. He was going to let her bite him, just like that? No need for subterfuge, no mind control for her victim—in fact, he claimed he was going to control her? She felt the strength of his mind as it brushed against hers, warm and welcoming, with a deep blue blush.

Take from me, Lady Nightwalker. Take what I offer freely.

Her hand trembled as she took his forearm and raised it to her lips. Apprehension faded as the aroma of his skin affected her the way it had on the dance floor. He smelled so good, so appetizing. She licked the skin across his wrist and savored him, swallowing a groan. So very, very good. He tasted even better than before.

Just on the outskirts of her mind she felt a mental gasp at the rasp of her tongue, and she realized he was more affected than he showed. He really wanted her bite, her fangs in his wrist sucking his blood.

His coaxing mental voice became a command. *Take from me, Cleopatra. Take what you need.*

No longer resisting, Cleo sank her fangs into his flesh and hot rich blood spurted into her mouth. She closed her eyes and swallowed the first few sips, the taste heady on her tongue. He tasted like nothing she'd ever had before. Tender, bittersweet with a little spice, like unsweetened chocolate with peppers. It reminded her of the Mexican food she'd eaten when still human. She couldn't help a moan of appreciation.

Simply delicious.

A rumble of amused mental laughter filled her mind. *I ate at La Cantina before I went to the club. I'm glad you like molé sauce.*

Like it? She loved it, and it had been so long since she'd enjoyed anything like it. In her mind came a memory of her last true meal, the night she was turned, also at a Mexican restaurant. Drinking from Michael was almost as good as the real thing. The heat of his blood hit her stomach and eased the cramps she'd been living with for so long they almost seemed part of her. Fulfillment rose, warming her and making her whole.

Something else grew warm as well, her central core heating with the influx of fresh blood, mixed with her awareness of him. Unconsciously she purred as she took more of his blood, feeling it slip down her throat.

His mind covered hers like a comforting blanket. *That's enough for now.* To her surprise a mental compulsion forced her to lift her mouth from his wrist.

Her first reaction was shock at how strong he was, mentally and physically, and she knew that without his permission she couldn't have continued to feed. Cleo stared at him, licking her lips and cleansing them of remaining blood.

"I'm still hungry," she said softly.

"I know," he said, his voice sympathetic, "but I want to get you back to my place. If you take everything you need now, I could be too dizzy to drive. I promise that you can have more blood later...as well as anything else you want."

His words were laden with sexual promise and it sent another shiver down Cleo's spine, cutting through her bloodlust. She could have anything she wanted? Thoughts of lying with Michael, enjoying his body as well as his blood filtered through her mind, enhancing her sexual desire even more than before.

Reluctantly, Cleo licked his wrist, catching the last few drops and sealing the wounds. There was no trace of her bite when she was done.

Michael's smile was thoughtful as he started the car and moved back onto the highway. "You feel better now?"

Actually she did. Her arm had ceased aching and when she checked the wounds they were half closed.

"What did you do? It shouldn't have healed that fast."

"I'm a companion...or at least I was until recently," he amended quickly. "My blood is special. Really good for growing nightwalkers."

"Oh." Cleo still didn't know what he was talking about. "So why aren't you a companion now?"

Michael shrugged, but she could tell he wasn't comfortable with the question. "My nightwalker met someone else. Someone special, so he had to remove his marks from my neck and let me go."

"I see," she said although she really didn't. How was it this apparently normal man knew so much more than she did about vampires? At least she assumed he must know something. Certainly his blood had done incredible things to her, healing her arm that way.

Even so it made her nervous. She was used to a simple life, quiet and peaceful.

And boring. Being with Michael was anything but boring. At the moment she liked that, but she also felt like she was at the start of a great adventure and if there was one thing she'd learned in her near hundred years of life it was this...

Great adventures got one killed.

Michael drove on and quiet descended in the car as they made their way deeper into Santa Monica and turned up the coast to where small houses and apartment buildings crowded either side of the road.

After about fifteen minutes Cleo wondered how far up the coast they were going when in a sudden move, Michael turned into a short driveway, and used a remote to open the garage door of a narrow three-story building on the coastal side of the highway. Soon the car slid into comfortable darkness, the inside of the garage dark once the door behind them slid shut.

"Lightproof," Michael said, indicating the space around them in the dim glow of the garage door light. "The whole place was built as a safe house back in the thirties."

Safe for whom, she wondered as she left the car and followed him up the narrow steps into the house. Not gangsters or spies she was betting, the usual kinds of people who needed safe houses.

Safe for vampires like her? She paused behind him as he used a key to unbolt the door at the top of the stairs, breathing deeply of his luscious scent.

One thing about it. Around this man she felt safe— except from him.

The large upper room was dark until Michael flipped on a wall switch and bathed it in the warm glow of several floor and table lamps scattered about the place. Another switch turned on narrow spot-lamps, illuminating the walls and a collection of framed artwork.

Artwork? Cleo's jaw dropped as she recognized what they were. Not artwork, but movie posters, and not just any posters.

Awed, she moved closer to the nearest one. A slender woman lay swooning over the arm of a large gorilla-like creature, her long blonde hair a stark contrast to the snarling monster's dark fur. Bold blood-red letters spelled out "Mate of the Monster" across the top, and in smaller but equally bold letters along the bottom were the words "Starring Cleopatra Lutz and Charles Devon".

Good old Charlie, she mused. She hadn't thought of him in decades. One of her favorite co-stars, usually in heavy makeup or some kind of animal costume, but that ape outfit had been his favorite. As she recalled, he'd been buried in it in the late sixties.

The blonde's face was, of course, the same as hers.

One by one Cleo examined the other frames decorating the room. Each was a movie poster in pristine condition from the late twenties or early thirties, primarily monster movies with a few gangster films thrown in. Outside of their age, the one thing they all had in common was her…each was for one of her old films.

Michael certainly had interesting taste in art and it was more than a little unnerving. Who would have thought she'd meet a fan…of her old films?

Her path around the room ended back at the *Mate of the Monster* poster. Michael stood watching her, his handsome face wreathed in amusement. "I've always been partial to this one. You look good as a blonde even if I do prefer your hair dark, the way it is now."

"It's naturally dark," she said. "The studio changed it for this picture, and a couple others."

"I think you've changed it a few times as well. Either that or you've worn wigs." He stepped up and his hands landed on her shoulders, stroking them gently. It was all she could do to not lean back into that warm strength behind her. Tempting as it was, she couldn't get too dependent on him.

Her primary purpose was to get his blood although if she could get sex as well, she wouldn't turn it down. It had been so long since she'd been in bed with anyone. He pulled her closer and she felt his erection through his pants. Long and thick, just the way she liked it, nestling into the crevice of her ass.

Oh, yes, she was definitely here for sex as well as blood. But that didn't mean she was going to get involved…no, not her, not with him.

"You had quite a career as an actress. What made you give it up?"

Even after all this time she couldn't help feeling bitter. Cleo turned and gazed up into his face. "I became a vampire," she told him, no humor in her voice. "That made it very difficult to make six a.m. rehearsals."

She expected him to draw away but he didn't. Instead he smiled and his finger traced her cheek. "You became a nightwalker," he said gently. "We don't use the 'v' word among the parafolk. It isn't polite. It's like calling a shapeshifter a werewolf, or a spellcaster a witch or warlock."

"Werewolves?" Cleo couldn't resist her snicker. "What do you take me for, a child? There are no such things as werewolves."

Michael's grin broadened. "Some of my best friends are shapeshifters. I'll be sure to let them know they aren't real the next time we're out for a beer. I'm sure they'll appreciate knowing."

His confidence shook hers. Did other kinds of—what had he called them, parafolk?—did they really exist? Rodriquez had never mentioned them, but then he'd told her there were no other vampires in Los Angeles. If Michael was to be believed, that clearly wasn't true.

It wouldn't have been the first untruth her maker had told her, Cleo acknowledged quietly to herself.

"What do you mean, 'we' when you say parafolk? Even if werewolves—that is shapeshifters," she corrected herself at his sharp look and proceeded more carefully, "and spellcasters existed, you aren't any of those things."

She stopped and suddenly wondered about his strength. Could Michael be as normal as he seemed? He did have heavy-duty psi powers.

There was certainly something abnormal about how much she wanted to throw her arms around him and drag him off to a bedroom. It was rare that she wanted to play with her food the way she wanted to play with him.

Michael leaned toward her, his mouth inches from hers. Cleo resisted the urge to meet his lips with her own.

He spoke silently to her. *I'm a psi, Lady Nightwalker. I have mental powers, and while I could have been a spellcaster with them, I prefer to be a companion. They make me an excellent companion. When I'm fed from I can control the link to keep your hunger under control. You never need to worry about bloodlust with me.*

She still didn't feel comfortable talking so to him through her mind. He was just too strong, too powerful. On the other hand, other intimacies were starting to sound pretty good. "What's a companion?" she asked.

Michael gave her a disbelieving look. "How is it possible you've never heard of companions? How long have you been in LA?" One hand indicated the framed movie posters on the wall. "Since then?"

One thing for certain, Cleo wasn't thrilled with how this feeding was going. She was used to being the one in control "Yes. Like I said, I became a vampire and had to drop out of show business."

"And the rest of the world as well, it seems." Michael shook his head. "Who was your maker, anyway?"

She wasn't going to tell him any more. "You don't need to know that."

Annoyance crossed his face. "Fine, keep your secrets — for now," he said, and it was her turn to be irritated. Michael acted like she would soon tell him anything he wanted to know…as if she would! After all, she knew how to keep secrets. She'd been doing it for far longer than he'd been alive.

He seemed to read her mood and see how displeased she was. He held up his hand.

"I apologize, Cleo. You have every right to not tell me. Here we've barely met and I'm rushing things…not to mention being a poor host."

With a rueful grin he stepped back and waved towards the living room and its overstuffed chairs and couches. "Let's relax and get properly acquainted. Why don't you make yourself comfortable while I rustle up some drinks? I bet I have something you'd enjoy…other than me, of course," he added, his grin broadening to show all of his perfect teeth.

Intrigued as to what he intended to serve her, Cleo ignored his suggestion to sit in the living room and followed him into the cozy kitchen nook in the corner instead. Her curiosity turned to surprise when he pulled a familiar-looking plastic bag from a medical supplier from the refrigerator and opened the narrow tube at the top, pouring some of the straw-colored fluid into a tall glass.

"I'm assuming you'd rather have it straight up for now," he said as he handed it to her. "It makes a good mixer for vodka, but I noticed you weren't drinking much at the club. Besides, I'd rather see you fed properly before you have much alcohol."

She sniffed it carefully. It was exactly what it seemed to be—cold blood serum, the fluid left over after the cells were removed from blood. Cleo took a tiny sip, letting the salty sweet fluid cover her tongue and smiled with surprise, only at the last moment remembering not to show her fangs.

So tangy! She'd never tried straight serum before but it was pretty good and it did quench some of her thirst. It didn't kill her craving for Mr. Tall, Dark and Delicious, but it did help.

Michael nodded approvingly as she took a deeper taste. "That seems to meet with your approval. You needed fluids, particularly with that wound."

"How do you know so much about my kind?" Cleo asked after they were finally settled in the living room. Michael opened the sliding glass doors that led to a deck overlooking the sandy beach and the ocean below. A cool breeze brought the clean smell of the water to her, and without thinking she relaxed deeper into the couch.

"You mean, how did I know you could drink serum? I've been living with a nightwalker for close to sixty years, I should know what sorts of things they drink."

Cleo choked on her drink. "Sixty years? But you don't even look like you're thirty!"

Michael played with the label on his beer, his eyes downcast. "Physically I'm not. Companions don't age the way normal people do. We live longer and are healthier. It's a reward for providing the blood a nightwalker needs, kind of a side-effect for carrying a mark and making more blood."

This was a part of her world she'd never heard of or even realized existed. "What is the mark?"

"The scars from the bite a nightwalker makes. Usually on the neck, but they can be other places. Haven't you ever marked anyone?"

She shook her head and Michael nodded. "Your maker probably taught you to remove them completely. That's what you do when you only want to feed from someone. If you seal but leave the marks, you leave some of the nightwalker DNA in the wound, and that causes the change of a normal human being into a companion."

He raised his head to stare into her eyes and she felt the heat of his desire for her but with a shock Cleo realized it was more than feeding her or sex that Michael coveted.

He'd told her that his master had found someone else and removed his marks. Obviously Michael had liked being a companion and wanted to become one again. If she didn't miss her guess, Michael wanted to belong to her.

Dismay made it hard for Cleo to swallow her serum. So much for a quick bed, bite and run. This guy wasn't interested in a one-night feeding — he was looking for a long-term situation.

Worst-case scenario he'd want to live with her like some kind of servant and she could barely support herself now. She tried to imagine him living in her little house. The place would be crowded and the last thing she needed was another mouth to feed.

When she'd become a vampire, keeping a low profile meant she'd had to disappear from the movie business. The best way to do that had been to move in with Rodriquez. In fact, the vampire had insisted she do just that.

She'd taken a few things from her home that she'd cared about and closed out her bank accounts, keeping the money close by to run with if she had to. As far as the world was concerned, Cleopatra Lutz retired into seclusion April 27, 1933, just four days short of her twenty-seventh birthday.

Not that it had been all bad. Rodriquez owned a beautiful home and she'd lived well there. They were sexually compatible, at least at first, and she'd had a couple of pleasant decades with him. He'd taught her to hunt, although she'd never been as good at it as he was. Rodriquez hadn't any scruples about using people for their blood while she always tried to make her victims comfortable. Her maker wasn't above causing pain when he fed.

Unfortunately, one night he'd run into someone even meaner than he was, ended up with a stake through the heart and had left her to her own resources.

Shortly after her maker's death she'd collected as many portable items of value from his home as she could manage and sold them before the estate had been confiscated for unpaid taxes. Between that and her savings, she'd acquired a nice little nest egg, too small to keep her in luxury, but with careful management it paid for the upkeep of her small home in Santa Monica and a steady stream of delivery boys.

She did miss the good life that she'd had and it irked her to realize that if she'd been able to collect on the income from her old films she'd be in even better shape financially. Every time one of her old movies ran on television it made her mad that someone else was getting what rightfully should be hers.

Unfortunately, she hadn't been able to find a way to collect what was owed her without documentation of who she was. How could she expect some bean counter in a studio to believe she was a ninety-nine-year-old actress when she barely believed herself?

A dealer in fake documents had gotten her a temporary identity that allowed her to work at the television station, helping her financial situation a little, but that wouldn't get her the residuals she should be earning. Too bad she couldn't pretend to be her own descendant, but a claim like that would need serious documentation to stand up to scrutiny. There was no way a studio money person wouldn't investigate a claim like hers and find every hole it had.

She glanced around at the understated and stylish beach house's living room. Obviously Michael was used to living much better than she was.

"This belongs to your master?"

"Kind of. It actually belongs to a foundation that pays the taxes and hides the fact that the real owner has been alive far too long. But Vlad lives here, with Samantha, now. It used to me my home before..." Michael halted before continuing with the same casual cheerfulness in his voice. Cleo wondered if he wasn't more bothered by his former master leaving him than he'd let on.

"I'm staying here until they get back. I guess I'll have to pack these up then and find a new place for them."

"Samantha is his new companion?"

"More than that. She's his bloodmate." With a movement she wasn't sure he was conscious of, Michael stroked his neck as if seeking something that wasn't there. He hesitated. "Vlad found someone he needed more than me and she meant more to him than I ever could."

Michael sounded more than a little wistful and it put Cleo on alert. "Nightwalkers sometimes develop relationships with…non-nightwalkers?"

"With their companions, sure. Nightwalkers aren't that different from anyone else. They fall in love." He shrugged as if the question didn't mean anything to him, but Cleo wasn't fooled. Michael wanted a real lover and that knowledge unnerved her.

In the many years since Rodriquez had died, she'd avoided anything resembling a relationship, fearful of what would happen when the man found out what she was. Now here was a man who knew and it didn't matter to him. He wanted her anyway—in fact, what she was seemed to be a bonus.

The uneasiness Cleo had felt from the beginning, when Michael had first pulled her onto the dance floor, solidified fully. Obviously Michael wanted to become her companion and of all the things she wasn't looking for, a human male who wanted a continuing relationship topped the list.

It didn't matter that she liked the taste of his blood or was intrigued by the strength and sensuality of his body. Sure she wanted to bed down with him more than any man she'd ever known and she had to include her maker Rodriquez in that list.

It didn't matter. The fact remained that he was someone whose mind was so strong she couldn't control him and who had plans for her she couldn't cope with. She appreciated that he needed a new place to stay and wanted to live with her, but she couldn't take care of him.

One way or another, she would have to escape from him.

It wouldn't be easy though. Coming here hadn't been smart — it would have been better to insist on a hotel room in town. It was too far past the full moon for her to fly and she couldn't drive. Belatedly she realized that by allowing him to transport her, she had no way to leave other than to call a cab, something that would be difficult to do without his knowledge.

Somehow she didn't think Michael was going to just let her leave without a fight. Not with the eagerly possessive way he was looking at her.

She should make the effort though. "You know, I really should be getting back home. How is the bus service out here?"

Her question startled him and he laughed. "Bus? There isn't any service to this part of town." He gazed at her curiously. "Cleo, there's no reason you have to go anywhere tonight. As I said, this place was built as a nightwalker safe house. It belongs to Vlad but he's gone at the moment and is letting me use the place. He and Sam are on their honeymoon." He smiled. "They took a long cruise to Tahiti, where the beaches are beautiful at night."

Tahitian beaches? Pure envy stabbed through Cleo. Wouldn't she love to take a long trip somewhere? It seemed like a century since she'd been out of Los Angeles.

Well, maybe only a little over half a century, but it felt longer.

"Anyway, there's a comfortable bed in a lightproof room I'll be happy to let you use in the morning and you can take your rest there until the evening. Assuming we haven't reached some other agreement by then."

Cleo took in the determined look on his face and knew just what kind of agreement he wanted, something about their sharing that comfortable bed in its lightproof room. Her body knew it too and seemed in happy concurrence with the idea.

Great—she got to fight both him and herself.

One thing for certain, if she stayed here tonight she'd probably not be going home tomorrow either. That adventure she'd been worried about would be well and truly under way and there'd be no going back to her safe status quo. Her only hope was to get out of here before things went too far. Trouble was that Michael seemed determined to keep her and even with her strength as a vampire the odds of overpowering him weren't good. She didn't want to kill him, after all.

At least she had one option to even the odds a little, a little something she'd learned to travel with when on the hunt. She gave him one of her most sensuous close-mouthed smiles and stuck out her empty glass. "This is so tasty. Could I have a little more?"

Michael grabbed her glass and, as she hoped, left his beer behind when he went to the kitchen. It was the work of a moment to slip one of the small capsules she carried in her purse into the bottle.

When he returned, he didn't seem to notice any change in his brew and Cleo breathed a sigh of relief. As she sipped her own glass, they fell into a safe conversation, about the movies, the ones she'd made in the days before she'd been turned and the ones he'd seen. It turned out he'd seen them all, several times, and owned most of them on VHS or DVD.

Michael regarded her with admiration. "You were so good, Cleo. It's a shame you quit when you did. You could go back to it, you know. I know people in the industry. Maybe we could even start our own studio, shoot only at night to accommodate your schedule."

For a second she let the idea tempt her before allowing reality to crash back in. "Those days are over for me. I do the

TV show because it's fun and I can get away with it. Besides, I need the money," Cleo laughed wryly into her glass. "I couldn't play a real part without smiling and the fangs are a dead giveaway. Besides I'm not even sure I could act anymore. It's been too many years."

A thoughtful look crossed Michael's face. "I bet you're as good as you ever were. As for the fangs, that's not all that hard to deal with. Some nightwalkers get false caps to cover their teeth when they're out in public. It reduces the effect of the fangs and gives you a more normal look. We could look into those if you like."

Again with the "we", Cleo thought, sipping her serum slowly. Michael was clearly planning their future together, whether or not she wanted it.

He gazed up into her face. "Of course I prefer your smile the way it is. It's sexy with those little fangs of yours just peeping out. They make me want to kiss you."

Michael took a last swig from his bottle, emptying it. Standing, he stalked towards her with a hungry look on his face and again Cleo wondered just who was hunting who here. Not since she'd been turned had she felt at such a disadvantage around a man.

Her heart sped up as he leaned over her, hands on the arms of the chair trapping her in her seat. Of course she wasn't really trapped. She could break free of him if she wanted to—she was still stronger and faster than he was.

But now he looked into her eyes and she was caught in the brown hypnotic depths of his. For a moment they stared at each other, feeling the heat rising between them.

He nodded towards her again empty glass. "Would you like some more of that, or can I offer you something more…substantial?"

From her vantage point, she could see his cock pressing large against the inside of his pants. Substantial wasn't even remotely the word for it. Sudden boldness made her reach out to stroke him through the fabric. Michael's eyes widened and he shifted his weight from foot to foot as if caught off guard, but he didn't pull away.

"Whatever my Lady Nightwalker wants she may have," he said quietly.

Oh, if only that were true. If only she could have him and her freedom too. Not that freedom from him was sounding as good as it had half an hour ago. She felt her determination falter a little. What could be so bad about spending the night in this man's arms? The drug she'd given him was subtle enough that he most likely thought it the beer he'd drunk.

She could go to bed with him, drink under his control and have what promised to be mind-bending sex with him. Michael stared into her face, his eyes full of promises. Anything she wanted she could have tonight.

And tomorrow night, and the one after that. She couldn't kid herself—she'd be under his control, as much as she had been with her maker. Michael's mind was too strong for her to overpower, even now when he was intoxicated from alcohol and the drug she'd slipped into his drink.

If she didn't leave now, she never would.

And that would be a bad thing? An annoying little voice popped into her head, making her wonder why she had to leave. Nothing waited for her but an empty house, an empty bed and a boringly empty existence.

Nothing about Michael was boring, the little voice argued.

Ruthlessly ignoring that little voice, Cleo reached for Michael's belt buckle. "Let's see what we've got here."

Eyebrows raised, he stood still as she opened his belt and then slid down the metal tab of his zipper. "And I thought you'd be shy," he said as she reached in to free his erection.

Oh, my… He really was a beauty. The breath caught in Cleo's throat as she contemplated his magnificence. Pure masculinity, perfectly shaped, and as big as she'd expected — an absolutely perfect penis.

It had been ages since she'd had one of these inside her. Damn… What a shame she couldn't act on her instant desire to impale herself on him and ride him into mutual oblivion. Unfortunately that wouldn't give her the chance she needed to slip away from the house and call a cab.

She couldn't have sex with him — it would have to be a blowjob only. Wouldn't do all that much for her but at least he'd enjoy himself. She'd think of it as payment for the blood she wanted and something for him to remember her by.

Leaning forward, Cleo tasted him, the sweetness of his skin coupled with the tang of the pearly pre-cum seeping from the head of his cock. She closed her eyes in near ecstasy over the flavor. Most excellent.

Michael seemed in near ecstasy as well. His hand cupped the back of her head and he breathed hard as she placed first one then another sensual kiss on the tip of his cock. Then she closed her mouth over the head, drawing him in, and he sucked in a deep breath. She didn't bite down but let the tips of her fangs slide along the soft skin, let them catch on the flared ridge.

He let out an involuntary gasp. "Cleopatra…"

Pulling his cock out of her mouth, Cleo looked at him sternly. "If you don't mind, I'd rather be called Cleo."

Michael gave her a shaky laugh. "Oh, Lady Nightwalker, whatever you want." He passed a trembling hand across his face. "But I've got to warn you, it has been a while for me and I'm most likely going to explode if you keep that up."

She stroked his cock from base to tip, running her hand along the thick vein she felt throbbing through the skin. "You've been my hero twice tonight and I owe you for that. It would be my delight to give you pleasure, Michael." She licked her lips, deliberately running the tip of her tongue across her fangs.

Some of his masculine need to dominate returned. "It's me who should be pleasuring you," he protested.

"There is no reason we can't take turns," she told him. "Why don't you lie down?"

He blinked as if dizzy. The drug must really be taking effect now. "Yeah, that's probably a good idea." He wavered and she had to help him lie on the couch. As he stretched out he nearly yawned. With an impatient hand he scrubbed his face, fighting his sudden drowsiness. "Damn, I didn't think I'd had that much to drink."

"Not to worry," she said coaxingly. "I'm sure you'll do fine." She stroked his cock with one hand, cradling his balls in the other. "Now just relax while I take care of you."

Apparently beyond further protest, Michael sank into the cushions while she went back to work on his lovely cock. Again Cleo started with the tip, letting her fangs rake a little deeper this time as she worked her way down the shaft. As she expected, he loved that, his back arching up.

Cleo couldn't resist a chuckle. Some things about men never changed. Rodriquez had loved having her fangs on his cock too.

Michael's skin was thinner though, and she'd scratched the surface, releasing a thin line of blood to seep from it. Cleo ran her tongue along the scratch, licking away the blood and erasing the minor wound. She'd have to be more careful. Hungry as she was, she didn't want to cause him pain or any kind of lasting harm. She just wanted to feed and get away from him before she was stuck. Unfortunately she could feel a good bloodlust coming on. The tiny amount of blood she'd gotten from the scratch had only whetted her appetite.

Good thing she had no intention of actually having sex with him. In her state it would be dangerous. She'd only take blood while she could control herself.

First she was going to distract him so that he didn't notice when she bit him. Michael twisted and muttered something unintelligible on the couch and again Cleo smiled, not bothering to hide her fangs. Fortunately in this condition he was easily distracted.

Using one hand to cup and massage his balls, she let the other play along his impressive length while her mouth continued to tease the head of his cock. Michael moaned but didn't interfere. He pulled his hands away from her, placing them on the couch arm above his head, giving himself completely up to her. His trust in her seemed complete. It was a heady experience having all that glorious male beauty to play with.

She could get used to having someone like this... Too bad tonight was all she would have. The traitorous little voice inside her grumbled over that and made another comment about her giving up a good thing, and in addition there was part of her that felt a twinge of conscience over betraying Michael's faith in her.

"Damn, Cleo. You are so good at that." He stretched like a cat against the cushions of the couch. "Yes, more please."

On the other hand, he wasn't exactly suffering, was he? She wasn't doing him any harm. No longer smiling, Cleo continued to lick and suck, one hand stroking the length of his cock, again and again.

Little licks turned into longer ones, her hand alternating short strokes for long. More than once she scratched him, and the faint taste of his blood mixed with his pre-cum, an appetizer better than anything she'd had before.

Michael's hands dug into the soft fabric of the cushions beside her. She felt him clutch and stiffen and knew his climax was coming. Pulling her mouth off the head, she laid a line of kisses down his cock, to his balls.

After giving them a good sucking that left him moaning, she found the place in his upper thigh where there was a vein close to the surface. While her hands continued to stroke him, she bit deep into his flesh, striking the vein, letting her mouth flood with his blood.

Oooo, so good. Arousal made him ever tangier than before with only a faint bitterness from the drug she'd given him. His was the best tasting blood she could remember, ever. She drank deep, not sipping lightly but swallowing as much as she could. She wouldn't risk his life, but she needed to take enough to incapacitate him for at least a day or so.

Michael stiffened again and cried out, his cock spasming in her hand. Sated, Cleo sealed the marks on his thigh and shifted to catch his cum on her tongue, licking him clean.

She groaned at the flavor. It was like having dessert. Amazing—everything about this man tasted good.

Michael seemed to take forever to recover, his breathing harder than she'd expected and concern hit her. Perhaps she'd taken too much blood? She tried to measure his vitals, pulling up his T-shirt and running her hands over his chest.

He opened his eyes, focusing on her face, his lips and perfect teeth in a wide, beautiful smile. "That was wonderful, Cleo. I can't believe how lucky I am."

Relief filled her when she found his steady heartbeat. She'd taken more than she'd intended, but he'd be all right in a few days.

"Lucky?" she asked.

"Lucky to find you." His voice was slurred but she could hear the sincerity in it.

"When I was a kid," he went on, "I saw all your movies. You were great and so very beautiful. And now look at you, still beautiful, and a lady nightwalker, alone with no other companions." He stroked her cheek with a gentle hand. "I could happily live the rest of my life with you, Cleo."

Much of it was the drug talking but Cleo couldn't help be touched. "Sleep now, Michael. We'll talk later."

Still smiling, he closed his eyes and drifted off.

Once she was sure he was unconscious, Cleo made certain she removed the marks she'd made on his thigh and cleaned up his cock with one of the kitchen towels. There were traces of blood on his pants but not on the couch.

Cleo let out an approving sigh. At least he wouldn't be mad about her messing up the upholstery. A colorful afghan lay on one of the chairs so she used that to cover him, tucking it around him so he'd rest comfortably.

There were still a couple of hours of darkness left when she closed the door to the house and walked outside to meet the cab she'd called. Time enough to get home before dawn came and she went into her own sleep as deep as Michael's drug-induced slumber.

As the cab pulled away, she looked back at the quiet little house on the beach, regret flavoring her enjoyment of finally having a full stomach.

Michael really was a tasty man. It nearly broke her heart to leave. But she couldn't stay with someone who would control her no matter how good they tasted.

As her maker had always told her, there was more to life than a good hot meal.

Chapter Three

** න**

Michael Brown sat in the front seat of his car, folded his arms and glared at the unobtrusive Santa Monica house as if it had personally offended him. Brick, mortar and wood, it didn't seem deserving of the dirty looks he was giving it.

Nor did it. In reality it wasn't the house he was mad at, it was the occupants.

Or, should he say, the occupant. Singular. Female. Nightwalker.

A singular female nightwalker who'd been in his arms three weeks ago, giving him the best blowjob of his life, taking his blood without his explicit permission and then leaving him to suffer the next day from one hell of a hangover due to the potion she'd dropped into his beer.

Oh, and one other little thing she'd left, a tiny present which was the first of two reasons he needed to speak with her, the other being pure revenge for eating and running the last time they'd "talked".

She'd claimed she was no longer an actress. Hah! She'd had him fooled completely, and after over eighty years of life that was pretty humiliating. Michael narrowed his eyes. She wasn't going to fool him again.

Preparations for tonight had taken him the better part of the last couple of weeks. After he'd recovered his wits, it had been the work of a few minutes to find out what cab company had picked up a fare in the middle of the night in front of his building then find out where the driver had taken her.

For a while he'd wondered if she'd covered her tracks by having the driver take her to a place other than her own, so he'd watched the house for several days. The first time a pizza delivery truck pulled up, he'd wondered if he could have made a mistake until he realized that the driver spent far too much time inside for someone just getting a tip. The bemused smile the driver had when leaving told him just how Cleo Lutz had been dining while living without a companion.

He'd watched for the next few days as a nightly stream of food delivery men had gone to Cleo's door only to leave nearly twenty minutes later similarly smiling. A check of Cleo's garbage showed where the actual food from her takeout dinners landed.

Scandalous, that's what it was. Some of those kids barely looked eighteen, too young to be blood donors, much less Cleo's dinner, even if she was biting them on the neck and not their privates.

He narrowed his eyes. It was bad enough she'd fed that way from him, but he'd be most displeased if he caught her doing it to anyone else. She might not think she belonged with him but he had no such illusions. She was his and his alone and in the future Cleo wasn't going to be biting anyone but him.

This was probably her idea of hiding out—keeping to her house and chewing on delivery boys. When he'd called to check on her next appearance on *Bloody Night*, he'd found that she'd even taken an extended absence from her television hostess job.

Just as well, since she wasn't going to be doing that anymore either if he could help it. He had plans for Cleopatra Lutz and they went beyond her working on a small-time TV show.

A delivery van pulled up in front of the house. Michael almost laughed when he saw the sign on the side, "Ming's Oriental Delights". So, she was in the mood for something exotic tonight.

Michael glowered with satisfaction. Good, she was going to get it—him, one order, "companion a la carte" to go. As he got out of his car to intercept her delivery, he wondered what she'd ordered. He hadn't eaten yet and was in a mood for shrimp fried rice.

The deliveryman didn't argue as Michael pretended to be the official recipient, collecting the bag and handing him the money, particularly after the other man counted the size of the tip. Michael smiled and watched from the step as the driver got back into his van and drove off before he turned and knocked on the door.

He held the bag with its distinctive logo over the peephole of the front door to hide his face, sniffing appreciatively at the aromatic smells coming from inside. Hmm, good—it did smell like fried rice.

He heard the deadlock on the door click and the door open. "Why don't you bring it in and put it down," he heard Cleo's distinctive voice say.

"Happy to, Lady Nightwalker." Pulling the bag away from his face, Michael brushed boldly past her and slammed the door behind him, blocking that way out.

"Michael!" To his amazement she didn't immediately run but tried to brazen it out. "What are you doing here?"

"I'm here because you forgot something the other night."

She crossed her arms, returning his glare. "And what was that?"

"Me. You forgot me. I'm your companion now." He leaned toward her. "It is very bad form for a nightwalker to not take care of her companion."

Shock and outrage radiated out of her. "You are not!"

"I am," he told her grimly. "You left your mark on me and that means I belong to you. Whether or not you want it."

Cleo honestly looked astonished. "I didn't! I was careful to leave no sign. I know it wasn't very nice of me to run like that but you weren't listening to me."

"Listen? What was it I was supposed to listen to? You didn't try to talk to me at all."

"I did...well, you just weren't in a mood to pay attention. All you wanted was me to take you on as a companion."

"And as it happens, that's exactly what you did, even if you didn't intend it. Trust me, Cleo, you left your mark. It may have been accidental, but it counts. You're just lucky I didn't file charges against you with the authorities. The Parafolk Council, and in particularly our chief, takes a very dim view of nightwalkers who run out on their responsibilities."

Her mouth gaped open. "What responsibilities? I didn't mean to take on any responsibilities. If I left a mark on you, I'll remove it." She looked him over, checking his neck for signs of her fangs. "Where is it?"

Michael chuckled. "Sorry, Cleo. It isn't as easy as that. I'm not going to tell you where you left your mark, but you can feel the effect for yourself. Check out my heart rate and blood pressure."

He grabbed her hand, placing it on his chest. She cringed as if touching him were somehow a problem for her, which didn't leave him feeling very positive. Then she straightened, tilting her head and listening.

"It's faster. Also your blood pressure is up. A lot."

Michael kept hold of her hand, forcing her to stay near him. "That's right. I'm a companion again, thanks to you." He held out his arm to her. "Ready for your use."

From her horrified expression, he could tell this wasn't the greatest news she'd ever heard. Now he knew how a woman felt after telling a man that she was going to have his baby. Cleo was not happy to have him as her companion, even if she'd been happy to take his blood earlier.

He tried to control his hurt. She'd drugged him and bitten him and left him behind when he'd told her he wanted to stay with her forever. It just wasn't fair.

Cleo couldn't believe any of this. It was like some horrible bad joke.

Michael had not only managed to track her down to her home, something she was sure he wouldn't be able to do, but he claimed that she'd somehow marked him. How was that possible? She was sure she'd removed marks of her fangs on him. After all, she'd only bitten him a couple of times.

The first time was on the wrist in the car. She could tell that wasn't it since he was again wearing a to-die-for tight black T-shirt and both his arms were mark free. Then later on she'd taken blood from his thigh, but she was sure she'd cleaned those up after he'd come in her mouth…

Oh, no. She remembered where else her fangs had been, the small scratches she'd made when she'd taken him into her mouth. But surely those were too small…

Or were they? Cleo's heart sank. She glanced at Michael's crotch then back at his face, fast enough to see his short-lived blush.

"Oh my god…I marked your cock?" Had she really left some little bit of her DNA in this man, marking him…on his cock? What a revolting situation that would be. For a moment she imagined herself in his place.

Imagine trying to explain marks on your privates?

Michael didn't answer her but his expression grew grimmer. Cleo remembered how he'd stroked his neck before as if looking for scars there. That would be the obvious place to leave a mark if you wanted to designate someone as belonging to you.

She resisted the urge to snicker. Maybe there was a reason Michael was reluctant to take his case to the Parafolk Council, whatever that was? Perhaps he didn't really want them knowing that she'd marked him on his cock without his knowledge. She imagined that might be an embarrassment to a big strong man like him.

Ignoring her amusement, he wandered into her kitchen, plopped the Chinese food on the counter and began searching the drawers. "I hope you don't mind, but I'm hungry. Being a companion makes you prone to eating more."

Again she resisted the urge to snicker as each drawer turned up as empty as the last. "You're looking for silverware in a nightwalker's kitchen?"

Michael fixed her with a glare then opened the bag from the restaurant. Inside were a pair of wooden chopsticks, which he promptly seized, split apart and began using with considerable zeal on the now open carton of fried rice. "Vry gud," he told her around a mouthful, his mood improving with each bite.

"I'm glad you approve," she told him. "I assume you intend to substitute for the driver I planned to have for dinner."

He grinned at her, flashing those perfect teeth. "Absolutely. I need a good feeding before I bust an artery somewhere."

She could use a good feeding too, but she wasn't so sure she wanted it from him. He was still too dangerous for her. Even so, she moved closer to him, to where she could smell his scent over the aroma of the carton of food in his hand. He smelled luscious, even better than she'd remembered, like all the best foods she'd ever eaten, rich and nourishing.

Her stomach growled and she had to resist the urge to jump on him, wrap her legs around his waist and sink her fangs in his neck, drinking from him good and deep. Cleo shuddered as the compulsion slid through her and shook her confidence.

Okay, perhaps she did want to feed from him. But that didn't mean she had to like it.

Michael crossed the kitchen to the refrigerator. "Any possibility you have some beer in here?"

As if. "I'm afraid not. Perhaps you should go get some," she said hopefully. Perhaps he'd leave and give her a chance to move her belongings. She didn't have all that much in the house, nothing she couldn't replace.

Well, except for the antique four-poster bed that was older than she was that she'd moved every time she'd changed homes and now kept in her windowless bedroom. It had belonged to her grandmother and she didn't want to leave that behind.

Oblivious to her thoughts Michael continued to study the inside of the refrigerator. "I guess you don't entertain much." He picked up a familiar-looking plastic bag. "So, I thought you hadn't had serum before?"

"I hadn't. I picked some up after we met." She shrugged. At least one good thing had come out of that meeting. She'd never thought to buy commercial blood products before. Now her refrigerator held an assortment of serum and even a few emergency pints of blood, as well as bottled water. She hadn't quite worked herself up to drinking vodka in serum as he'd suggested, but it was on her list of things to try.

With a smirk that told her Michael knew he was responsible for her increased variety of beverages, he grabbed a bottle of water and closed the refrigerator. Boosting himself on top of the kitchen counter, he opened the bottle with a swift twist and took a deep swig. Everything this man did, he did with such enthusiasm. It was exhausting.

Watching him sit on the countertop, Cleo had a brief irrational moment when she wished she owned a kitchen table and chairs, or at least a tall stool so that there was someplace in her kitchen to sit. Other parts of the house were furnished…not as nicely as the house Michael lived in, but a vampire…that is, a nightwalker, didn't use the kitchen much and she suddenly realized how forlornly empty hers was.

"So, shall we discuss the situation?" Michael asked.

"What situation?" Cleo asked, stalling for time.

"The one we're in, my lovely nightwalker. How you drugged me, seduced me, made me your companion and then ran away after I'd done nothing more than save your beautiful butt from harm twice."

Cleo flinched. She didn't remember the situation quite like that, but guys always did have their own point of view. "Would it help if I said I was sorry?"

He paused in mid-swig from his water bottle. "Actually, it would. Are you sorry?"

She was now. "You have to understand, Michael. You came as a complete surprise to me. One minute I'm all alone in the world then there you are, telling me that others of my kind exist as well as a whole society of parafolks, and you're trying to convince me to take you on as a companion. It was a bit overwhelming."

He grinned, obviously enjoying her description of him. "Okay, I can see that. I overwhelmed you." He jumped off the counter and stalked towards her. "Do I still overwhelm you?"

Well, duh! She tried not to shrink away from him. "A little."

Looming over her, he stared down at her. "If that's the case, then why are you standing here? You're a nightwalker, Cleo. You should be faster than me, stronger than me. Why don't you run away?" He leaned closer. "Unless you want to be with me tonight?"

In spite of herself, Cleo backed up against the wall. "What good would running do? You'd just chase me down later. There isn't anyplace for me to run to, not if you could find me here."

Michael shook his head. "I was afraid you were thinking that way. I want you to want me as your companion because I'm the best thing that could happen to you. I also think I can prove that to you…if you'll give me the chance. Are you going to do that?"

She'd been a nightwalker on her own for too many years to agree so fast. "I think you'd do or say anything to get me under your control."

"I wouldn't really control you, Cleo. Just feed you and be there for you. Don't you think I could be an asset?"

She raised her chin high in the air. "I've been doing all right up to now. Why should I allow you to be part of my life?"

Michael rested his hands on either side of her head, leaning forward as if he intended to kiss her. He stayed that way for a moment, studying her face, and Cleo wondered what he was looking for. Trust? Desire? Love?

Could Michael really want her love more than he wanted a position as her companion?

She stood up to his scrutiny, hoping her face wouldn't give anything away. She knew she wanted to have sex with him. Trust and love? That was a completely different subject. It had been a very, very long time since she'd trusted anyone and she couldn't remember when someone had earned her love. Maybe never.

His frown told her he hadn't liked whatever he'd read in her face. Still, he shrugged as if it didn't matter.

"Very well, Cleo. I'll make a deal with you. If you can get away from me tonight, then I'll let you go free. You can remove the marks you left and I won't ever bother you again."

Her heart pounded harder. "You'll let me go free?"

"Only if I can't find you in," he studied the clock on the wall, "let's say about two hours. I'll even give you a five-minute head start." He grinned at her. "A children's game, Cleo, easy enough to play—Hide and Seek. If you can hide from me for two hours, then we'll call things quit. I'll agree that you can take care of yourself and don't need me for the job.

Cleo glared at him. "I don't need you to take care of me."

"Of course you do." Michael said with more confidence than she felt. "You're living without any kind of daytime protection and eating delivery boys. I've never seen a nightwalker more in need of a companion than you are. Think about it, Cleo. If I could find you here then anyone could, including the Watchers. Their leader Phinious Jones would love to get his hands on a real live nightwalker to prove the parafolk exist."

Michael sobered and he reached out to take hold of her chin. "Believe me, Cleo, you don't want to get caught by that bunch."

Cleo felt a surge of fear. She had been surprised that Michael had found her but hadn't really considered the implications. To date she'd used her anonymity to shield her but that could be compromised now.

Michael released her and with a grin folded his arms. "So you have one chance to prove that I can't find you. Otherwise you'll have to try things my way and keep me as your companion for a few days. Just until the next full moon and I'll let you go."

His grin grew even more confident. "I'm betting that by then you won't want me gone. Either way will be good for you. Does that sound fair?"

"You're serious? If I can elude you for two hours you promise you'll let me free of you?" This was too easy, there had to be a catch. "How do I know I can trust you to keep your word?"

A deep sigh erupted from him. "You doubt me, your unsworn companion? Okay, I'll put it into writing and sign it. It will be a binding document that you can take to the Council should I give you any further trouble. Take it with you and if I can get it back in two hours, then I'll win."

He leaned closer, inches away from her face, and she could feel the heat of his breath on her cheeks. "I'll even throw in a bonus. Since I chased away your dinner, you can feed from me before we start."

He was so close she couldn't help but catch his scent, a heady mix of soap and shampoo, the Chinese food he'd eaten, plus something else, very definitely his own aroma. From the beginning Michael had been the most appetizing man she'd ever met and that hadn't changed. Her mouth watered at the thought of drinking his blood again.

It would be the last time, of course. Given a head start, there was no reason she shouldn't be able to elude him for at least a couple of hours, if not all night.

Cleo took a deep breath, filling her lungs with his smell. Arousal woke, just as it had the last night she'd spent time with him. For a moment she thought about making love to him as she fed. Not that anything was going to happen tonight, any more than it had before.

"First write the agreement and sign it," she told him. "Then we'll see about my feeding. I think you need me as much as I need you."

With a flourish Michael pulled a folded piece of paper from his pants pocket and handed it to her. "I took the liberty of putting this together ahead of time."

The paper did say what Michael had agreed to. Cleo read it aloud. "I, Michael Brown, do state that if Cleopatra Lutz can elude me between eight and ten o'clock tonight, then I will free her of any obligation to me. Otherwise she must give me until the full moon to establish our relationship before leaving me." It was dated and signed and looked perfectly legitimate.

She glanced at the kitchen's clock, which showed seven-thirty. "It seems all right," she said slowly.

"So do we have a deal?" He held out his hand.

She took his hand and shook it, ignoring how warm it was and the thrill just holding it gave her. "You'll give me a head start?"

"From the time you finish eating until eight. I'm afraid you'll have to make do with a straight companion feed this time though. No fancy sex games."

"Sex games?" Cleo said indignantly. "I don't play sex games with my meals. I put them into a trance and take from their wrists, then remove the marks so no one notices..." Her voice trailed off as she remembered what she'd done with him. "Oh, you were thinking about what I did to you. You were different."

"I was?" For a moment Michael looked pleased. "I'm glad to hear you don't treat all your meals to a blowjob. Speaking of which…"

He stared at her meaningfully and she backed slowly away. Surely he didn't mean for her to go down on him this time. She wasn't really in the mood…had something of a headache… Okay, she just didn't want to do it…right then. Maybe later.

A lot later.

Michael only needed one step of his long legs to catch her. With a single tug he lifted her and sat her on a nearby countertop, pushing her legs apart so he could stand between them. Leaving his hands on her hips, he pushed close to her, and she could feel the power of his erection through his pants. For a moment Cleo wondered if he intended to kiss her, but then he tilted his head, exposing his strong, muscular neck.

"It's time you were fed, Cleo." He brought one hand up to cup the back of her head and urged it gently towards him.

Take what you need, my nightwalker. I offer freely.

Cleo steeled herself against his compulsion, but then realized it wasn't a command this time. She could start feeding or not if she wanted to, but he was leaving it her decision. Cleo breathed in his delicious aroma and her mouth watered. All that luscious blood, hers for the taking. She leaned in closer and ran her tongue along the length of the vein, felt it throb. She smelled his excitement at her touch.

For the first time she spoke into his mind. *You really want this.*

She watched him swallow convulsively, his Adam's apple bobbing at the unconscious action. He turned his head and his brown eyes stared into hers, a longing in them that he couldn't hide.

Yes, I want this. Feed from me, Cleo.

With gentle precision she placed her fangs over the pulsating vein in his neck and bit down sharply. Blood burst into her mouth, filling it, and she had to swallow quickly to avoid spilling.

Michael made the briefest moan but held perfectly still. She didn't have to suck. With his blood pressure so high the blood poured out of him and all she had to do was hold it in her mouth and swallow. He tasted even better than she remembered, a hint of exotic spice flavoring the blood.

A little like shrimp fried rice. For a moment Cleo wondered if she was experiencing his memory of the carton of food he'd just consumed. Odd, she'd never done that with one of her meals before.

Even faster than she was used to, she'd had her fill. With a single swipe of her tongue she closed the wounds and a second swipe removed their evidence from his neck.

Michael leaned against her, his breath hot against her cheek, his mouth a whisper away from hers. Hesitantly she reached for his mind and found it awash in desire, deep purple need coloring his usual mental shades of blue.

"I thought I told you no sex stuff," he said heavily, his breathing hard. Even after her feeding his pulse rate was up far higher than it should be.

"I didn't," she said. "That is... I didn't mean to."

He growled and captured the lobe of her ear with his teeth, tugging on it slightly. "I suppose you can't help it. Or we can't help it. We're drawn together because you need blood and I need you, but there is more to it than that. We want each other as well. There is always going to be that tension when you feed from me." He leaned back and the look in his eyes was pure passion.

For an instant Cleo was as hot as he was, and her mind turned into flame. Thoughts of being with him, lying with him, making love with him and feeling that cock of his deep inside overwhelmed her.

It was so tempting. They could head for her bedroom, close the door and she could lose herself in his arms.

Michael's face brightened. "You want me as much as I want you. Why don't we skip our bargain and simply spend the rest of this evening in bed getting to know one another better." He gave her a devastatingly sexy smile and rubbed his hands along her back. "That four-poster bed of yours sounds really good."

Her bed? He was reading her mind without any help from her! This man was too, too powerful for her to manage and that realization doused the flames of desire in her. She pushed him away. "No."

For an instant she read disappointment on his face then his easy grin was back. "Very well, Lady Nightwalker. I guess we'll just have to do this the hard way."

He reached up his hand to touch where her fangs had been. "You could have left the marks, Cleo. I'd rather be marked there than...elsewhere."

She liked how smooth his neck was without the scars. "What difference does it make where the marks are?"

His eyes burned hot. "A companion carries his nightwalker's marks with pride, Cleo. They are the sign he belongs to him...or her."

"But I don't want you to belong to me!"

"You do...but you don't know it yet. I need to convince you to keep me." He glanced at the clock. "Okay, Cleo, it is now seven forty-five. I'm going to give you until eight as a head start. If you can elude me until ten, I'll let you remove the marks you left on me and you're free."

She grabbed her purse and stuck the folded agreement in it and headed for the door. "How do I know you won't follow me for fifteen minutes?"

Michael shook his head and sat again on the countertop. "Cleo, you have no faith in people. I give you my word I'll stay right here."

Something was fishy, but she couldn't figure out what it was. Michael was just too confident. She could be halfway to the airport and a late night flight to San Francisco by eight. Not that she had any intention of doing any such thing.

Oh no, not her. Michael might even expect her to do something like that, but she had her own plan for how to outwit and elude him. Something he'd never imagine.

Cleo almost grinned thinking about it but remembered her fangs just in time. Sometimes people got weird when she smiled broadly, even if Michael had said he liked her teeth that way.

She moved towards the door. "You'll lock the door before you leave? I wouldn't want to have to eat any burglars on my return."

A bright confident smile was her answer. "Not a problem, Cleo. I'll lock the place up good and tight because you won't be returning here tonight. Once I find you, you're mine."

Right... "Okay, I'll see you around." She headed out the door and slammed it behind her. Then she sneaked back and peeked into the kitchen window to see if he really was planning on staying put.

Michael still sat on the counter and he waved at her through the window, an amused smirk on his face.

Arrogant son of a... Well, no need to finish that thought. She only had fifteen minutes to make herself impossible to find. Turning, she headed for the street and made a left, walking fast until she knew she was out of sight of the house. Then she began to run as fast as she could, first down a cross street, then back along another, heading the opposite direction. She doubled back again and this time leaped a fence and began running silently through backyards instead of going along the street.

She came to a school, deserted at this time of night, and she cut across the playground, past the swings and slides and other equipment. Her only observer was a dog that loped with doggie nonchalance well behind her on the opposite side of the street. Otherwise no one was around to watch her mad dash for freedom.

Once she was past the school, she took another left turn and headed for Wilshire, one of the major streets in Santa Monica. Even if Michael could track her this far, he'd assume she was going for some kind of transportation to take her out of the city, but she bypassed the bus stop and even let a cab go by without hailing it. Instead she continued to run until there was too much traffic and too many curious eyes to do so.

Slowing, she walked down Wilshire, keeping a close watch for anyone on her tail. For a moment she thought she saw someone watching her, but it was a young woman on a cell phone and as Cleo watched she headed into a nearby store, still gabbing away at whomever it was she was talking to.

Cleo shed a sigh of relief. At least she was sure Michael wasn't anywhere around. Even if he'd been able to get to his car right after she'd left the house, he couldn't possibly have followed her during her suburban steeplechase. He had to be looking for her where he'd predict she'd go.

She'd covered pretty close to five miles in the ten minutes since she'd left the house and that gave him far too large a search area to find her. Maybe he'd expect her to find a culvert to hide in or an abandoned building. He certainly wouldn't expect her to hide where there would be other people around.

Soon her destination was in sight, one of the small retrospective movie theatres on Wilshire, which as it happened tonight was doing a set of two old *film noir* movies. Thankfully neither was one she'd starred in—otherwise he might have guessed she'd go there.

The theatre marquee was bright and welcoming, and Cleo felt right at home when she paid for her ticket and entered the lobby. She gave a brief sigh over not being able to purchase the delicious-smelling popcorn or a soda, instead settling for bottled water. Oh, well, she told herself, it was healthier for her anyway.

At least this time her stomach was relatively happy, having had Michael to dine on. The best meal she could remember in a long time...actually, since she'd taken his blood at the beach house.

Ruthlessly, Cleo censored her pleasure in remembering how excellent Michael's blood was. She didn't want to become dependent on her so-very-temporary companion for anything, including his blood—even if it was delicious, nutritious and everything else he'd said it would be. He'd made it clear she'd have to take him as a full-time companion and give up her freedom to have it and that price was too high for such dining.

The first feature was just starting so she found a place in the nearly empty back half of the theatre and settled into the comfortably worn red plush seat. Music swelled and the title came up on the screen, and she leaned back, happy, once again in her favorite environment. In the anonymous shadows of the theatre she felt safe again.

As the opening credits finished, Cleo grinned, letting the darkness hide her fangs as she thought of her "companion" searching fruitlessly for her in the city outside.

She opened her water and took a deep appreciative sip. *Catch me if you can, Michael.*

Chapter Four

ᴆꙎ

On the wall-sized screen, the tall dark-haired man straightened his three-button suit and glared at the blonde, her hair shining silver in the black and white print.

"Frankly, doll, I don't care about your problems," he said. "I've got enough of my own."

The blonde wrung her hands. "But you must help me, Charles. If Todd finds me, I don't know what he'll do."

Enthralled, Cleo sipped her water and mimicked the woman's lines. Not a bad delivery, but she could have done better. She remembered reading the screenplay, *Guns, not Roses*, when she was a working actress. At one time she'd been up for the role of Donna, the "fallen woman with the heart of gold". It was a juicy part and she'd have loved to play it. Unfortunately Rodriquez had come along before she could be cast and the rest was history.

Cleo tamped down that old resentment. It didn't matter anymore. After all, the actress who had gotten that juicy role was dead now and here she was…still alive and as youthful as ever.

Still alive, for all the good it did her. It wasn't like she could do juicy roles now. Smothering a sigh, Cleo leaned back in her seat.

The smell of buttered popcorn wafted over her, setting her mouth watering. Cleo closed her eyes. Oh great, that's all she needed. One of the reasons she liked the weekday evening shows at the Old Art Theatre was that the fewer patrons meant not having a lot of appetizing inedible smells around to plague her. She even sat in the back to keep away from other people.

The smell came closer and Cleo realized that its source was in the row behind her. She heard someone settle into the seat behind hers and a heavy crunch as a handful of kernels went into their mouth.

Wonderful. Cleo looked at the virtual sea of empty seats around her. Why did the person with the popcorn have to sit right behind her? It just wasn't her night.

She leaned forward, hoping to avoid the worst of the smell and crunching, and tried to focus on the movie instead.

So, did I miss much?

Cleo froze in place, her heart leaping into her throat. She'd know that mental touch anywhere. Michael! How could he have found her here this quickly without following her?

"What did you do, read my mind to know where I was going?" she whispered.

"SHHHH," came a loud voice from four rows in front of them and Cleo cringed in her seat. So much for being inconspicuous.

Better to talk mentally so we don't disturb others. And I'm not going to tell you how I found you. What would be the fun in that?

Michael leaned forward and held the bag in front of her. *Would you like some?*

She was rusty at mental communication, but she didn't want to draw any more attention than they already had. *No. I can't eat popcorn. I can't swallow it and the kernels get stuck in my fangs.*

He gave a quiet chuckle. *Wouldn't you like to know what it tastes like?* His mental voice held immense amusement and it made her want to hit him.

Not if it means kernels between my fangs. Those hurt!

She heard his audible sigh. *Open your mind a little, Cleo. Relax and let me in, just for a moment.*

Unsure of his intentions but curious anyway, Cleo let the edges of her mind open up, feeling the blue of Michael's merge with hers. He took another few kernels of popcorn and slipped them into his mouth.

Salty flavor mixed with sweet butter cream filled her mouth then she felt the satisfying crunch of popped corn against her tongue. Without thinking, Cleo closed her eyes and just appreciated the taste and sensation broadcasting from Michael's mind into hers. He chewed slowly, drawing out the moment before finally swallowing.

She opened her eyes in amazement and turned in her seat to stare at him. *What did you do?*

Gave you a glimpse of what life with me will be like. When our minds are linked, you can taste what I taste.

Can all companions do that? Send to a nightwalker's mind?

No, not all. It is actually rather rare, he admitted. *I wanted to see what would happen if we tried.* He didn't broadcast more, but even through his confidence, she could see that Michael had been more than a little surprised at how successful his experiment had been.

For a long moment they just sat and faced the movie with unseeing eyes, Michael apparently as lost in his thoughts as she was.

What did it mean that she could merge minds with him so thoroughly that she could taste his food? Most likely something he considered good. How she viewed it remained to be seen.

She really did need to know more about this whole companion/nightwalker business.

So, shall we continue this elsewhere, or are you really that interested in the movie?

The truth was her interest in the movie had disappeared long ago, somewhere between Michael's sudden appearance and her first taste of movie popcorn. But she wasn't about to let him know that.

Who says I'm going anywhere with you?

You promised you'd cooperate with me if I could catch you. You are well and truly caught, Lady Nightwalker. Why don't we go someplace where I can show you just how good that can be?

Sensuous purple threads traced through the blue of his mind, leaving her with images of them lying together in a soft bed. Warm hands caressed her in ways only he could imagine them doing, holding her breasts and tweaking her nipples and sliding between her thighs to play with her clit.

Cleo thrilled as he broadcast his thoughts to her. Naughty, excellent thoughts. Some of the ideas Michael had were positively decadent and well beyond Cleo's limited experience.

It would be so easy to say yes to him. Michael always made it seem easier to say yes than no. But she wasn't about to give in to him. *I didn't actually promise anything. You're the one who promised to let me go if I could elude you. I didn't disagree, but I didn't say I'd stay with you if you did catch me.*

Michael settled back into his seat with an audible sigh. *I was afraid you were going to be difficult. Very well, if that's the way you want it.*

Suddenly feeling in danger, she leapt to her feet, but he grabbed her from behind and forced her back into the seat. His hand slid to the back of her neck and she felt a needle-like pain. Almost immediately she felt faint.

"What did you do?" she whispered, whimpering a little as molten heat entered through her veins, suddenly making her limbs too heavy to lift. Her water bottle slipped from her hands and onto the floor, rolling into the row in front of her.

Nothing you didn't already do to me first. Go to sleep, Cleo. I'll take care of you. I promise no harm will befall you at my hands.

She didn't even have a chance to cry out. His mental promise was the last thing she knew.

After slipping the drugged dart back into his pocket, Michael changed rows to the seat next to Cleo and sat with his arm around her, letting her unconscious head rest on his shoulder. She seemed so frail like this, and for an instant he worried about the dose he'd given her.

Perhaps it would be too much for her? He might have been irritated with her, but he didn't want any lasting harm to come to her. Anything but!

But no, she had his blood in her, and companion blood should protect her. She might have a little bit of a headache in the morning but given the one she'd left him with on their first meeting, he didn't feel too guilty about that.

Having his blood in her might also keep her from staying under very long, which meant he probably should get her out of here before anyone noticed. Regretfully, he left the rest of his popcorn on the seat next to him and took a long draw on his soda before abandoning it as well. Slipping her purse under his arm, he pulling her arm across his shoulders and half-lifted, half-carried the unconscious nightwalker through the empty back of the theatre to the emergency exit door that emptied into the alley.

As he'd planned, his car waited for them, a teenage girl standing near the open driver's door, watching for trouble. She had a cell phone clipped to her belt but for once wasn't actually using it.

Her jaw furiously worked a huge wad of gum and she gave him a toothy smile when she spied Michael, opening the back door so he could carefully place his burden across the back seat.

"So, you had to do it the hard way, I guess?" she asked, snapping her gum with practiced relish. "I could tell she wasn't going to go easy, not with the chase she gave me."

Michael grimaced. "One thing about Cleopatra Lutz, she's predictably stubborn. Thanks for taking care of the car, Tammy. Did you have any trouble?"

The girl grinned, showing lots of very straight and sharply pointed teeth. "Trouble, me? No, more's the pity. It would have been fun. I was in the mood to take apart a carjacker."

Resisting the urge to comment on how shapeshifters had an unusual sense of fun, Michael pushed Cleo's body into the corner of the backseat and fastened her there with the seat belt.

Tammy watched his efforts with definite amusement. "You know she's a bit on the puny side for a nightwalker. I'm not sure I've ever seen a nightwalker as little as her before."

"Perhaps not." Michael considered Cleo for a moment then grinned. "Not much meat on her, but what's there is *cherce*," he said in a bad Brooklyn accent.

The young shapeshifter rolled her eyes. "Another movie quote, huh."

"Yep, youngster. Old movie, before your time."

"Well, she's small but she can run pretty fast. I had to push it to keep up with her, and when she started jumping fences, I almost lost her a couple of times."

"Coming from you, I'd say that's high praise. I'm glad you approve of her."

"Oh, I wouldn't go that far. She's okay for a nightwalker."

Finally satisfied that he had Cleo as secure as possible, Michael climbed behind the wheel while Tammy took the passenger side. She blew a big pink bubble before fastening her seat belt.

"I appreciate your help tonight, Tammy."

"Good." She gave Michael a long look of speculation. "You know, I was thinking. You aren't paying me a lot for this job. I wonder if Chief Jonathan wouldn't take a pretty dim view of kidnapping her."

Michael glared at her. "Tammy, I don't like being blackmailed."

The girl grinned. "So what are you going to do about it?"

For a moment Michael considered his answer. "Well, for one thing, I remember your dad complaining about all the money he spent on braces to get your teeth aligned. Didn't he once say that he'd lock you up for a week the next time he caught you chewing gum?"

Tammy's eyes widened. "You wouldn't fink on me."

"Only if you fink on me first, shapeshifter. I do unto others what they do to me—you remember that from now on."

Michael glanced at the unconscious nightwalker in the back seat then picked up her purse and removed the folded agreement he'd made from it, putting it into his pocket. "You can bet that Ms. Lutz will be remembering it in the future."

Chapter Five

ഔ

The next thing Cleo knew was waking to her body announcing the sunset, just as it had the past several decades. In a ritual she'd gone through every evening since viewing her last sunrise, she yawned and stretched to work the kinks out of her back. But when she tried to pull her arms over her head, she found that her hands were bound loosely to her sides, and her waist roped to the edges of the narrow cot beneath her. She tried breaking the rope, but it must have had a silver core—she couldn't even stretch it. At least the cotton casing protected her against the silver.

She groaned. *Michael and his games.* Yesterday was Hide and Seek, today's seemed to be Tie Up the Nightwalker. Who knew he'd be into anything as kinky as this?

Well, more than bondage was involved in this game. This was abduction, pure and simple. He'd caught her, drugged her and hauled her out of the movie theatre to wherever this was. At the time Michael had spoken of taking her somewhere so they could work on their relationship.

This must be the place. Cleo sat up as best she could and tried to check out her surroundings. Unfortunately, looking didn't do her a lot of good, even with her super night vision. The room, if that was the proper name for the space around her, was as dark as a crypt.

Oh, heavens. He hadn't put her into a tomb, had he? She tried a short sharp cry then listened to see if she could tell how large the area was. The echo took time to come back and was muffled when it arrived.

Cleo relaxed somewhat. Okay, wherever she was, it wasn't a tomb, unless they made tombs the size of a warehouse and lined them with some sort of soundproofing. There was at least a lot of open air around her.

She gave the bindings on her wrists a good tug before giving up. They'd be tough to break but not impossible. At the very least she could untie them with her teeth, if she didn't mind taking a chance at cracking a fang on the silver core of the rope.

For the moment she left them in place. Michael had tied her up because he wanted her to stay put and for the moment she'd humor him. He'd made a deal to release her in three days if she let him behave as her companion during that time.

It seemed that ropes were going to be part of the relationship he wanted. She should probably get used to being tied up.

A shiver of anticipation slipped through her and she groaned. Damn it, why did that have to turn her on? Somehow everything to do with that man had a tendency to make her think of sex. In seventy years of being a vampire — or nightwalker, as he liked to put it — she'd rarely thought about making love as often as she did with him.

Of course he was the only male she'd spent any significant time with since Rodriquez had died — maybe that had something to do with it. Having an available man around could be a factor in her interest.

A soft rustle came from the darkness near her then she smelled Michael's distinctive musky scent, right before he sat on the cot next to her. Immediately her heart went into overdrive and she had to suppress another groan.

Nope, it wasn't just his availability that was making her horny, it was the man. She'd want him even if he were hard to get. Thank goodness he didn't seem to be hard to get at all.

Are you awake, my nightwalker?

Given her current train of thought Cleo couldn't help a sensual shudder at Michael's mentally projected question. His powerful mind touch felt like a caress, like a hand running along her body, stroking from her head to her...well, to parts of her that hadn't been caressed in a very long time.

She answered his question with one of her own. *Where are we?*

She felt his pleasure the second the thought was out of her mind and regretted it, both bespeaking him and the use of the word "we". Now he would think she thought of them as together, and she didn't. She really, really didn't. It was just a slip of the mind, but one that revealed far too much. She'd be better off avoiding bespeaking him.

"Why don't we talk aloud, Michael?"

In the darkness she saw the white of his smile. "We are in my new secret lair. I selected it just for you and it's where I intend to reintroduce you to yourself. I picked the perfect place for it."

"Secret lair?" Curiosity overcame her and she tried to sit up, forgetting the ropes. She tugged on them in irritation, and Michael reached over her to remove them. With a few quick movements, Michael freed her, rolling up the bindings as he did.

A very tidy man—even with his ropes.

"Sorry about tying you up, but I didn't want you wandering about until I was here."

"Why?"

He picked up a remote control and aimed it at the ceiling. "Oh, because I knew it would take you a while to find the light switch and I didn't want you to hurt yourself in the dark. At the moment your low-light vision is probably a bit impaired from the drug I gave you."

He pressed a button and the entire ceiling lit up, revealing the space, as she'd predicted, to be anything but an underground crypt. Cleo startled then smiled as she recognized her surroundings. It was like an empty warehouse, but one with a ceiling of heavy girders to support lights and backdrops, and with heavily padded walls. Near to them were empty camera stands, portable lights, reflectors, fans and similar equipment.

"A soundstage? How on Earth did you get access to one of these?"

"We're on the old Eagen Brothers lot. It's been abandoned for years, but I know someone with the key. No one ever comes here and at first I thought it would simply be a good place for us to be alone. But then I saw you in the theatre last night." He moved closer to her and Cleo tingled all over.

"I watched you doing the lines from the movie and I remembered how you were once up for the role of Donna. It was a shame that you didn't get the chance to play it. You would have been great."

She couldn't help her blush of appreciation at that, even if it was useless. "That's all behind me now, Michael. Even if I wanted to be an actress, assuming I could find someone who would let me work only at night, and I could hide my fangs as you suggested, I'm old and way out of practice. It's been so long I doubt I could even remember lines anymore."

"You are only as old as you feel, Cleo, and believe me," he ran his hand down her cheek, "you don't feel old at all. It is never too late to do the things you love. I want to prove that to you." He opened up a bag at his feet and pulled out several bound sheaves of paper. From her experience she recognized them immediately.

"Scripts?" she asked. "Where did you get these?" She glanced at the title page of the first one. "*Guns, Not Roses.* This is the screenplay of the movie last night."

"I thought you'd like to take a stab at it yourself, Cleo. It's a good part, a strong female character with a secret past. Not unlike yourself."

She couldn't help her laugh. "And I suppose you'd play her gangster lover?"

Michael lifted his handsome chin. "I once did a little acting. Bit parts, but I wasn't that bad. What do you say, Cleo? It will be fun. Something to do together."

She gestured around the empty soundstage. "So we'll just act out the parts here, by ourselves?"

"For now. I talked to some people last night and they'll be here later to help with cameras and mikes." He grinned at her. "This is Los Angeles...a lot of movie buffs and would-be film people around here, even among the paranormal community. Unfortunately not all of us can work in the business because of who we are."

Michael stood and looked around the soundstage, his quick gaze taking in the empty quiet. "That's something I've been thinking about. Imagine this place filled with people like us, those who are shut out from the rest of the industry. Shapeshifters, nightwalkers, spellcasters and psi folks like me, with too many mental powers to really fit in with the norms."

Opening his arms wide, he gestured at the vast space around him. "We could open our own studio, Cleo. We could make films for our people, as well as commercial movies for the rest of world." He gave her a grin. "Imagine how much we could save in special effects and makeup by going natural."

She wanted to scoff at the idea but Michael was so earnest, she couldn't. It was impossible, of course. The whole key to survival for a vampire was to stay out of the limelight and a movie studio for paranormals could hardly exist by residing in the shadows. And that was assuming people like shapeshifters existed…something she'd believe when she met one.

Even so, she could appreciate his dream and wouldn't deny it to him now. At the moment she had bigger things to worry about, like how she was going to get away from him so she could feed. Even now her stomach rumbled uneasily.

Michael spun around and grinned knowingly at her, as if he'd heard her belly complain. "You hungry, Cleo?"

"Not that much," she said, a louder growl interrupting and belying her words and Michael's grin widened at her expression.

"Oh, I see. What kind of noises does your stomach make when it is hungry? Those must be something if this is 'not that much'."

"Maybe if you have some of that serum I could have that."

Michael moved back to the cot to sit next to her. "Why would you want serum when you could drink from me?" he said, his voice a soft suggestive croon. A small thrill went up Cleo's spine at the sound.

"I drank from you yesterday. It's too soon…"

"Not for a companion," he interrupted her. "That's one of the reasons for having someone like me around, Cleo, so you have a regular source of food."

Her jaw dropped in astonishment. "Regular as in daily? No one could keep up with that kind of drain. It would be fatal."

"To a normal human, that's true, but I'm not exactly normal, Cleo. I'm a companion and I produce far more blood than I need. I can feed you today without trouble and I'm sure tomorrow as well. After that, we'll see. Remember that I told you there are companions who are their nightwalker's sole source of nourishment."

"Wouldn't the nightwalker get bored eating from the same person all the time?" The instant the words were out of her mouth, Cleo regretted them. Michael's eyes flashed angrily at her.

"Do you think a man would get bored with having only one woman to make love to? Is feeding any less intimate than sex?"

It had never been intimate for her, but then she'd never done anything but casual feedings. But every time she took blood from Michael, casual didn't seem to figure into it. As for sex… Whenever she thought of sex and Michael, sensual tingles ran down her spine.

"Some men do get bored by monogamy. Some women do too."

He shook his head. "Only if the relationship is flawed. There is never anything boring about sex, or feeding, when it's done right." He moved close enough so she could smell his rich blood through the surface of his skin. Cleo's mouth watered and she swallowed quickly to avoid drooling onto her chin.

Michael ran his hand down her arm, capturing her hand in his. He pulled it to his mouth and kissed the back of it. "I can assure you, Lady Nightwalker, that no nightwalker has ever tired of my taste. As for sex… I'll move heaven and earth with the right woman. You'd never grow weary of me."

Heat poured though her and centered in her core and she couldn't help leaning closer to him. "You think I'm the right woman?"

He leaned forward to kiss her, his lips soft against hers. But then they grew harder as he pulled her closer to him and she felt his solid chest beneath his T-shirt. Michael's tongue slipped past her fangs to delve deep in her mouth, tasting her.

Cleo couldn't remember the last time she'd felt a man's tongue in her mouth. She'd avoided French kissing since becoming a vampire—that is, a nightwalker. It was just too difficult to explain the fangs. She'd forgotten how good it felt…and this man felt particularly good. Michael's kiss was wonderfully different.

The way everything was different with him.

It was frightening how different things were. It wasn't just that she'd been pulled from her routine of takeout dinners and self-imposed obscurity. When she was with Michael she found she wanted more than what her life had become, hiding in the shadows, afraid of discovery. Sometimes she wanted the better life he offered.

Sometimes she wanted the great adventure. And that was scary—that she might want more than what she had, that the status quo wasn't good enough for her anymore. She felt as if she were on the first steps of a journey that would take her someplace uncertain. It worried her that it would be hard to go back should she find the better life Michael promised came with a price tag she wasn't willing to pay.

Ignoring how much she wanted to continue, Cleo ended their kiss and pulled away from him, but Michael didn't seem bothered by her withdrawal.

Instead he smiled at her knowingly. "I bet you're really hungry. Why don't we get you fed?"

She was hungry all right, but not necessarily for blood. More than bloodlust was in her—real lust was involved too. Michael's kiss had left her wanting for more than what ran in his veins…she wanted his body.

Fortunately, Michael seemed remarkably comfortable with sharing intimacies with her. In fact, from the look in his eye he was probably more comfortable than she was with the idea.

He took the back of her head and urged her into his neck. His skin lay just below her mouth. When she breathed in, his scent flooded her nose and her mouth watered even more. All she had to do was lean forward, bite down and take it. His blood, hers for the asking, a meal offered without lies and subterfuge, provided by a willing donor.

Again he didn't touch her mind to compel her to take his blood as he'd done before. This time he simply waited, allowing her to decide if she'd accept what was given freely.

Who was she to turn down an offer like that? Cleo bit into his neck.

A small gasp was his only reaction to her. His heart sped up but not too much as she pulled in the first mouthful. Sweet and warm, and infinitely tastier than any human blood she'd had to date—that was Michael. The fact that he permitted—no, not permitted, welcomed her bite—made the whole thing surreal...and oddly nice.

Nice wasn't something she was used to, but a part of her was wondering if she couldn't learn to like it. There was something just very...nice about drinking from Michael. It was like it was normal in a world that she'd long ago decided held no reasonable measurement of normalcy for her.

She took another deep drink from his vein. Oh yes, delicious—tasty and warm and cozy as a familiar meal, the kind her mother had made when Cleo was a child. She could certainly get used to this. Imagine having a regular blood donor as her own special comfort food. Cleo could easily become comfortable with Michael, at least as far as feeding from him was concerned.

As for sex...Michael's hand wandered down her back to her ass, caressing her butt cheeks gently. Even as she drank from him he drew her closer, pulling her into his lap so her crotch lined up with his, the juncture of her legs flush with his now obvious erection. In one quick movement he slid his hard cock between her legs, rubbing her most sensitive parts with his.

Oh my, yes. She could really get used to this. She tried rubbing back, but his hands on her rear held her firm, keeping her still. She could feel his mind reach for hers, the haze of his thoughts now more purple than blue.

His hand moved up to caress the back of her head and the mental thought he sent her held amusement as well as passion. *You know what I said about avoiding sex with your meals? Now I'm certain that's impossible with us. Sweet Lady Nightwalker, is there more I can offer you than what's in my veins?*

Trying to carry on a conversation with her mouth full wasn't something Cleo was used to doing. Throwing caution to the winds she sent him her answer mentally. *There seems to be something in your pants I might find interesting.*

He laughed, the sound resonating in his chest. Momentarily distracted from her feeding, Cleo sealed and erased the wounds on his neck and leaned away from him to stare into his eyes. *You think I'm funny?*

Hot desire stared back at her. *I think you're wonderful, Cleo. Make love with me.*

Waves of desire set up along her limbs and moved into her pussy as she grew hungrier for his cock than his blood. Her nipples peaked, hardened and ached for someone's touch…no, not just someone. Michael's touch. She wanted Michael to touch her.

As if reading her body as well as her mind, his hands sought her breasts and lifted them, his thumbs caressing their pointed tips through her shirt. Cleo moaned and leaned closer to him, giving him better access.

"I've wanted you from the moment I saw you," he whispered.

And she him, from the minute he'd rescued her in the bar...not that she'd ever tell him that. There were some things that Michael didn't need to know — at the very least he didn't need the extra encouragement that kind of admission would give him. The man was too confident in their relationship already.

Still, what he'd said gave her the thrill of a very long lifetime. Cleo couldn't remember the last time a man had told her he wanted her, knowing what she was.

That's what seventy years of being out of circulation did for you. Made you vulnerable to the least little thing...like being wanted as a woman. She'd fended off would-be lovers in the past, but they hadn't known what she really was and if they had they'd have headed for the hills.

As many years as she'd seen as a nightwalker, she hadn't once had a human lover. Her maker had warned her to avoid them. He'd told her that it was too difficult to avoid bloodlust during sex. If she bit her partner she'd take too much and her lover would die.

That was the reason Rodriquez had given for turning her into a vampire without her knowledge. Of course, he'd also told her that he was in love with her and couldn't live without her, but she'd soon realized that what he'd really wanted was a ready sex partner.

For years she'd performed that function with him, believing he was her only choice of lover now that they were the same. He'd never told her there were others like them nearby or she might have sought them out.

Their sexual relationship had been as much an inducement to keep her living with him as the safety of his home had been. A virtual army of servants, never staying too long in her maker's employ, had provided a steady source of nutrition and they'd rarely had to hunt for their meals. Cleo had been comfortable, both with him and their life together.

But then Rodriquez had lost interest in sex with her and hunted for cheap sex among those who were expendable. She had no idea how many women he'd killed, but one night he made a mistake and had taken a woman who'd been missed.

That had been what had gotten him killed, looking for love in the wrong place and earning a silver dagger through his heart as a result.

Cleo had learned from Rodriquez's lesson and avoided normal men and their temptations.

But Michael was anything but a normal man. He wanted her as she was, in spite of what she was...maybe even because of what she was and he saw nothing abnormal about it.

Suddenly she needed to feel human again. "Make love to me, Michael. Make me feel like a woman."

His slow smile held so much heat it nearly singed the hair on her head. "Oh you are a woman, Cleo, make no mistake about that." He pulled her closer into his arms, again rubbing his intriguingly large package against her crotch. "I could never see you as anything else."

She felt herself smile broadly enough to show her fangs. "Just a woman with odd teeth and an even odder diet."

He laughed again. "Not so odd to me. I've not known a lot of lady nightwalkers, but the few I did know were women first and nightwalkers second." Leaning in, he lifted her chin and stared into her eyes. "You needn't think that I view you as a bloodthirsty monster."

She almost melted under the warmth of his stare.

Then he grinned at her. "Besides, like I said, I think your fangs are kind of cute."

Now it was her turn to laugh and it felt good. The blood he'd given her rested warm in her stomach, the taste of it lingering on her tongue, but he treated her like she was an ordinary desirable woman.

Michael Brown was a very dangerous man, if only because she could get so very used to having him around and she worried that would be a bad thing in the long run.

Wouldn't it? She wasn't as sure as she had been of that point. Right now his presence seemed very good and after all he'd promised to only keep her for three days and to free her at the end of that time. What would be the harm?

Cleo found herself wanting those three days with him, to test the relationship he told her they had.

Even as she debated what to do, Michael took action. With a strength she found surprising for a human, he flipped her effortlessly onto her stomach and began rubbing her back, making the movements slow and relaxing.

"What are you doing?" she asked.

"You're too tense to make love just now and I want you to enjoy yourself. When was the last time someone gave you a backrub, Cleo?"

Had anyone ever given her a backrub? She couldn't remember, although that might be because with the way he was caressing her she was having trouble remembering her own name. She groaned aloud as he touched and soothed a particularly tense muscle. "That feels so good."

"It's supposed to," he purred into her ear. "It would feel even better if I had your clothes off."

Pulling off the T-shirt she'd worn the night before and her bra only took a few seconds and then Cleo lay face down on the cot again.

She heard Michael laughing and looked up to see why.

He couldn't seem to help his merriment. "At least I found an efficient way to get you undressed."

"Oh, shut up and rub me," Cleo growled at him without rancor. At his touch her growl turned to a purr, and then she was too involved to make any noises but those of pleasure.

Sure he was a dreadful tease, but he could tease her all he wanted if he'd just rub her back this way. Or that way. Or any other way for that matter. She wasn't that particular as to how she was rubbed at the moment.

He used long strokes to free her muscles and made her skin tingle. Once again Cleo noted what talented fingers Michael had. Many, many years of practice, she guessed, and for an instant she felt a certain amount of jealousy over the number of women he'd probably used those fingers on.

"Relax, Cleo," Michael whispered in her ear. "No sooner do I get you loosened up but you tense up on me."

She couldn't help her biting reply. "You do this to all of your lovers?"

Michael's hands stilled. "I haven't had a real lover in a long time, Cleo. I'm not sure I even know what it would feel like." A wistful tone entered his voice. "I watched Vlad and Samantha together…they were lovers almost from the beginning. Sometimes I wish for the same thing, that kind of closeness."

He moved his hands to the base of her spine and returned to massaging her lower back. "Maybe someday we'll grow that close. Closeness requires trust and I think that's as hard for you as it is for me. We probably need more time to really know each other well enough. Fortunately we have plenty of that—time, that is. In the interim I'd settle for you accepting me as your companion."

Michael found all of the sensitive spots on Cleo's back and played with them until she was nearly limp on the cot.

Limp but not relaxed. Unfortunately, as good as this backrub felt it wasn't doing a thing for her pussy, that empty place inside her that had been wanting a man for far, far too long.

The backrub had been great, but she needed a different kind of rubbing now.

Cleo turned over and pulled on the front of Michael's pants. "Enough pre-foreplay. Let's get serious."

He grinned and pulled off his T-shirt, revealing a sturdy masculine chest, just enough muscle development to be interesting without overdoing it. He only had a little body hair in just the right places and Cleo's fingers ached to play with the brown hair that outlined his nipples. She nodded approvingly, reaching out to let one hair curl around her finger. "Nice."

"I'm glad you like it. I've never been one to enjoy shaving my chest."

As her fingers played with his chest hair, he unbuttoned his pants with very deliberate movements, opening his fly one button at a time. To Cleo's amusement and delight, he wasn't wearing any underpants.

Freed, his cock thrust proudly forward. Cleo took a preliminary glance but didn't see the fang marks he'd claimed she'd left on him. Perhaps if she looked closer... She leaned forward.

Michael pushed her head away. "Oh no you don't. No removing those marks until you give me proper ones. I like being your companion and I want to stay that way. No oral sex until I can trust you."

She licked her lips and tried to look hurt. "You mean you don't want me to lick your cock at all?"

He seemed indecisive for a moment and she knew his dilemma. She'd never known a man who didn't enjoy having a woman's mouth on his cock. Finally, he shook his head reluctantly. "I think I better say no to that for the moment. We need to get things clear between us first."

He leaned over her and she felt oddly vulnerable. He was much bigger than she was and was more powerful than a normal human even if he did lack her innate strength as a vampire.

Cleo eyed his muscular arms warily. She could take him in a fair fight. Probably.

But then he shook his finger under her nose and she wondered if she could.

"You will not remove the marks even if you find them," he said. "Not for the next three days. After that, if you still want to leave, I'll show you where they are and you can take them off. But until then we have a deal."

She still had trouble taking him at his word. No one, not even her maker, had ever played things straight with her. "You'll really let me go?"

"I said I would, didn't I? You've never had a companion before so you don't really understand what it means. If I can't make you see the advantages of keeping me around, then I don't deserve to be with you. In the meantime…"

He lay down and covered her, his lips fastening to hers in an intense kiss. It was a kiss of possession, one that as much as said "mine", but for once Cleo was in no mood to worry about his possessiveness.

Heat blossomed through her veins, as warm as his blood in her stomach. Cleo couldn't mind Michael's kiss. She wanted him too much—his body and his blood. There would be time later to set him straight on where their relationship stood.

For now all she wanted was to surrender to him. And surrender it was. Michael's arms encompassed her, boxing her in and trapping her against the mattress. There would be no escape…they were going to make love, right now, on this bed, whether she wanted it or not.

Oh, yeah, like she was going to say no at this point. She couldn't be less interested in disagreeing with him and from the grin on his face when he lifted his head to stare into her eyes he knew it. He rubbed his engorged cock against her thigh.

You and I are in complete accord, Lady Nightwalker.

Sitting up, Michael undid her belt and the top button of her pants then lowered the zipper slowly, drawing the moment out. He lifted her and pulled off her jeans, letting them fall to the side of the bed. Now all that was between them was her underwear, pale green silk. For a moment he stroked her through the crotch, milking her folds and clit until her underpants were damp with arousal. He pulled those off and they joined her pants on the floor, then Cleo lay naked on the bed, Michael equally naked with her.

He knelt between her legs and spread them gently with his knees. Liquid heat pooled inside her pussy, and she watched as Michael collected some of it and lifted it on his finger. He put that finger in his mouth and licked it, his eyes registering his pleasure at the taste. She moaned a little as he sucked her cream from his finger, noting the way his tongue curled around the tip, the way she imagined him doing on her clit.

He smiled again as if he read her thoughts. Maybe he was…heaven knew she wasn't hard to read right now. For a moment he paused, letting his hands run down the outside of her legs, moving to cup her ass and raise it into the air.

Raise it to his mouth. Michael closed his lips over her clit and sucked hard, and Cleo's hips rose off the bed. "So good!" she moaned

"Good? You have no idea how good it's going to get!" And then he showed her with his mouth and hands just how good Michael could be. Cleo continued to moan as each lick and nibble sent shock waves of pleasure through her.

She realized he was giving her every bit as good oral sex as she'd given him in his home weeks before. Could she ever give him up after this? In some ways he was binding her to him, just as she'd bound him, but with desire and not vampire marks.

Finally when she thought she could take no more, Michael rose over her and stared into her face. She expected him to speak but he used his mental voice instead, probably wanting to drive home how intimate they were.

I'd like to spend more time exploring you, but I've waited too long to have you, Cleo. If I don't take you now, I might strain something.

She couldn't help her laugh at the ironic tone of his thoughts. *I know what you mean. Please, I want you.*

Then you will have me. He fitted his cock to her slick and open core and surged forward, sheathing himself deep within her. "Cleo," he breathed aloud, his audible voice harsh with need and want.

Oh heavens he felt good. Big...very big. With his cock buried inside her she felt fuller than ever before and the feeling was awesome.

Michael stared down into her face, his face showing his own astonishment at how wonderful their joining was.

This was very, very bad. She could get far too used to this.

Don't worry, he thought at her, a slight smile on his lips. *I might be addictive but I'm not harmful. In fact I'm just full of what sweet little nightwalkers need to stay healthy.*

At that implicit invitation Cleo pulled his head closer, leaning in to lap gently at his throat. Michael shuddered, the skin quivering against her tongue. *Take what you want from me. I'd give anything for you.*

She couldn't help her teasing reply. *Anything? That could mean a great deal, Michael. You should be careful what you promise.*

I will never promise more than I can deliver, Lady Nightwalker, to you or anyone else.

His self-confidence seemed complete and who was she to argue? It had been decades since she'd been with a man at all, much less anyone like him. If Michael wanted to deliver satisfaction, she wasn't going to object.

Making love was making her hungry and he was clearly inviting her to indulge her appetite. With a quick movement she dug her fangs into his neck. Michael made a soft moan of pleasure but didn't stop her. Cleo took a deep satisfying drink just as Michael began to pump slowly into her. For long moments she sucked as he stroked, both of them taking pleasure.

Tasty as his blood was, Cleo loved having his cock in her even more. She removed the marks she made on his neck and leaned back to better focus on making love with him. She met his stroke by raising her hips and each time they met sparkles of pleasure raced through her. Had she ever had a man like this? If so, she couldn't remember when.

No one compared to Michael.

I'm glad you think so, came his amused thought.

Cleo could hear the male satisfaction in his mental voice and knew he'd caught her last thought. Damn his mental powers anyway! She'd have to be more careful about what she thought around him — that was for certain.

Not really, my precious nightwalker. You can think all the good things you want about me — I really don't mind hearing them.

His smugness was absolutely too much. *Well, I mind that I can't have bit of privacy in my own thoughts*, she rejoined, letting him feel her irritation. Michael laughed and sped up his stroke, sending even greater sensations into her, and Cleo's irritation melted away in a sensual flood. He surged deeper and she couldn't help her heartfelt moan as he reached deeper places that had gone untouched in the past.

She loved the push and pull on her pussy as he drove deep within her.

A rumbling, possessive growl escaped Michael's throat. His mind was a purple haze where it met hers with virtually no trace of its usual calm blue. Cleo gave in to the urge to link with him and experience his mind gripped by sex. She felt his surprise at her boldness even as he opened completely to her, welcoming her into his mind. It was wild and passionate, full of crazy sensual imaginings like miniature pornographic films, all of them starring her.

Cleo blinked at some of what she saw. *Why Michael, you have a very dirty mind!*

You are...inspirational...

She laughed but her amusement fled as pressure built inside her, powerful and intense. Her skin tingled, nerve endings firing in waves along the surface as Michael's big hands caressed her. He wanted her. He'd wanted her for a long time and he had her now. Cleo felt his joy in that, both in his body and his mind.

She belonged to him...and him to her. That's the message his mind sent her in bright colorful bursts along with his sexually driven thoughts. Cleo reeled under the assault, both mentally and physically. Their mental connection overwhelmed her and she drew back from him, separating their minds just as a massive orgasm overcame her, swamping her mind and body in ecstasy.

From what seemed like a great distance Cleo heard Michael cry out, a guttural sound as much animal as man. His cry held pleasure, yes, but there was also a hint of loss in it. She felt his cum shoot within her and flood her pussy with its heat. He collapsed on top of her, his weight trapping her onto the bed as if he could keep her there with him forever.

When he stared down into her face, she saw a trace of anger in his expression. "You didn't have to pull your mind away when we came. The connection wouldn't have hurt you, only made things better."

Chapter Six

ℰᴐ

Michael couldn't help his disappointment. He'd sometimes joined minds with the women he'd made love to and enjoyed it thoroughly even though the link had never lasted long enough for them to reach completion. Two psis could join minds but it was rare they could hold the link as long as he and Cleo had. The link between companion and nightwalker ran at a different energy level than that of the more casual link two psis could manufacture.

But never had a woman cut him off that way, and it hurt that she'd done it just as they'd reached orgasm. They could have shared climaxes, something that his former nightwalker, Vlad, had raved about after he'd found his bloodmate.

If they'd stayed joined he would have experienced what Cleo felt during their lovemaking. She'd pulled away as if she hadn't wanted him to have that knowledge.

"I didn't mean anything," she told him, her voice small. "It was wonderful."

At Cleo's look of dismay, he fought how hurt he felt. After all, this was new for her and he'd probably overwhelmed her again. He seemed to be making a bad habit of that.

"I know. It's probably been a long time since you had sex with someone in your mind and you weren't ready for it."

"I never did that before. My maker..." her voice broke off and she turned her gaze elsewhere. "I don't want to talk about that. Having sex with you wasn't anything like being with him."

Some of his bitterness faded away at the pain in her voice. "I guess I'm glad of that. You did enjoy yourself."

Her eyes turned bright with laughter and she even grinned enough to show her fangs. "Oh, it was magnificent!"

He joined in her laughter and the last of his resentment disappeared. At least the sex had been great even if she had pulled away. At least she'd initiated the contact with him, something that had surprised and pleased him immeasurably.

The next time would be even better—and there would be a next time to make love to her. He knew that without a doubt. Even now he could see her sidelong glances as they dressed, the raw sexual interest she had in him.

She liked drinking his blood and enjoyed making love with him. That he knew for a fact. But she still seemed reluctant to commit to a real relationship with him in spite of all the benefits having a companion would give her. How was he going to overcome that reluctance?

Sex was at least part of the answer, and her hunger certainly helped.

For the rest... He hoped the idea of doing movies again would provide the answer. She'd been too long alone and cut off from what she'd enjoyed doing most. When he'd watched her in the theatre, he'd seen the intensity in the attention she'd given the screen.

At one time performing had been as great a need for Cleo as food and sex. If he could give that back to her, he had another argument for her making him her permanent companion.

It would give him something as well. For years he'd been living from day to day, not really thinking about the future or making plans for it. Once he'd realized how many years he had in front of him, worrying about what to do with those years had faded in importance.

It wasn't like he was concerned about money. Being Vlad's companion had given him many opportunities to accumulate wealth and he'd taken advantage of them early on. The nightwalker had provided the means in the form of his already considerable savings from the past several hundred years, trusting Michael to invest it.

For some time Michael had spent his mornings at restaurants and similar places where the high rollers in business tended to hang out. Reading their minds had given him enough information to know what to invest money in and when to buy and sell stocks.

He'd kept their activities cautious, investing small amounts at a time and spreading them around to avoid notice, but over the years he'd amassed a considerable fortune in both his and Vlad's interest, enough to keep both of them comfortable for the rest of their lives. Both of their lives, which given the nearly unlimited life expectancy of nightwalkers and their companions promised to be a very long time.

Even now Michael liked to drop into a particular coffee shop where certain developers of the latest game technologies liked to hang out on Saturday mornings... Their minds were most illuminating and sometimes very profitable. He'd cleared over a hundred thousand dollars this year alone.

Profitable as it was, making money so easily had stopped being as fun as it had been. He might as well go to Las Vegas and read the minds of the blackjack dealers, although cheating at cards had its own set of difficulties. Early on, the people who operated professional gambling operations had seen the benefits of hiring parafolk.

If he tried it he'd most likely be up against a fellow psi keeping watch for the casino security, and end up banned from Las Vegas for life if he got caught. That wouldn't be any fun at all. As a result Michael made a point of only playing the slot machines when gambling. He almost never could predict their payoff enough to win too big.

Any more than he could predict Cleo.

Michael had been thinking of going into business for himself for some time now. He was ready for a new challenge. Excitement rose as Michael contemplated his tentative plans.

He'd start with winning Cleo and then think again about the idea of opening a movie studio. Maybe they could call it Fly by Night Films or something like that.

Distracted by his thoughts, he missed it when Cleo picked up the top script from the pile he'd left and started leafing through it. When he looked over she was sitting in one of the folding chairs, deeply engrossed in the manuscript, her forehead furrowed in concentration.

"This is good," she said. "Even better than I remembered."

Her enthusiasm made him smile. He might actually be onto something with this movie business idea as a way to win her heart. "So do you want to run through a few scenes?"

She put the script down and gave him a long measured look then shrugged. "If you're going to keep me here against my will then I guess we could. It will be something to do."

"You aren't a prisoner, Cleo, at least not exactly. But since you've inadvertently made me your companion I thought it best that you not leave until we work things out." He took a deep breath, worried how she might take this next bit of news, but he had to tell her for her own sake. "By the way, I rigged things up so you can't leave here."

He'd been right to be concerned. Cleo's eyes narrowed at him. "What do you mean I can't leave?" She glanced suspiciously at the nearby exit doors, well marked and clearly unblocked. "What did you do?"

Her obvious anger made him question how good an idea this had been, but better to face the music now than later. "I sort of booby-trapped the doors," he said carefully. "I strung up lights outside all of them—strong UV lamps, set to go off if you open the door. You could get a nasty burn but they won't kill you," he added quickly.

Her eyes narrowed even further. "And when were you going to tell me about your little surprises? After I tried to escape and exposed myself?"

Michael cringed. "I was going to tell you, Cleo, but I didn't have the time. You haven't given me much of a chance to say anything."

She didn't look the least bit mollified. "We had enough time to have sex. Under the circumstances there should've been time for a warning about trapped doors."

Michael considered. Cleo had a point but admitting it to her would give her an advantage he didn't need her to have. He had to be strong or she'd run right over him...and then out the door. It was time to let her know he wasn't going to let her trifle with him anymore.

Leaning over, Michael fixed Cleo with his steadiest glare. "You've run out on me before, first at my place after drugging me, and you tried it again at the theatre when I succeeded in finding you. I think not trusting you only prudent under the circumstances, and I think I'm entitled to take steps to keep you here. You'll be fine so long as you stay where I want you to stay."

Sniffing in disgust, she returned to perusing her script, but Michael thought he detected a bit of respect in her attitude. He resisted the urge to smile. Cleo might still be ready to flee at any moment, but at least she now knew how determined he was to keep her. Smiling to himself, he picked up his own copy of the screenplay and turned to the scene he'd marked ahead of time to study the lines of the male lead.

There were plenty of battles left to be fought, but at least he'd won this round.

"Frankly, doll, I don't care about your problems...I've got enough of my own." Michael delivered the line with all the gusto it deserved and Cleo resisted the urge to smile at him, an action not in the script.

Instead she wrung her hands as the manuscript directed. "But you must help me, Charles. If Todd finds me, I don't know what he'll do."

Doing his best "Charles, gangster without a soul" imitation, Michael leaned closer. "Well then, Donna, I guess you better find some way to convince me to care. You haven't given me any reason to put myself out for you." He ran his hand along her cheek and leered suggestively. "Perhaps if you put your mind to it you could think of something."

Cleo didn't have to fake the shudder of desire that went through her at his touch. In character or not, Michael had that effect on her. All she had to do was say the lines...the acting wasn't hard at all.

Not when she wasn't really acting.

She put a little bit of a tremble into her voice. "What do you want of me, Charles?"

"Oh, I think you know what I want, doll. In fact I think you want the same thing." He leaned over to capture her lips in a soul-searing kiss that left both of them too breathless for the next lines.

They stared at each other for several long moments before Cleo's mind recovered enough to return to the script. She picked it up and made a point of finding the next line, running her finger along the page. "Why Charles...I didn't know you felt like that…about me, that is. I didn't know you wanted me." She stumbled over the words like the character would have, but it wasn't only being in character that caused her to do so. Michael's kiss was potent.

He growled, and that was potent as well. "Yeah, doll… I want you. I want you to belong to me, and no other. I take good care of what I have. So if you want help, all you have to do is ask. I'll do it… But afterward you'll be mine, once and for all."

As Donna would have, Cleo tilted her head to one side, as if weighing her options. The situation in the screenplay wasn't all that different from Michael and her circumstances. Michael wanted her to belong to him…or at least for them to belong together.

The similarities were distracting and she had to force herself to stay focused on the script. It would be too easy to give him what he wanted, the same as Donna was doomed to give Charles. Every time Michael leaned into her she smelled his special scent. The flavor of his blood was still on her tongue and it fired her interest in other things.

He would let her bite him and make love to her again… All she had to do was ask. It was heady having him so available. If she weren't careful she'd give in to him and give him what he really wanted, even if it meant giving up her freedom.

Suppressing a sigh, Cleo returned to the script for her next line. She nearly laughed when she found it. It was inevitable.

She flung down her script and threw her arms around him. "Whatever I have to offer, Charles, you can have. I'm yours." She kissed him, long and hard.

After a few moments, she broke away from the kiss. "Aren't we supposed to fade to black?"

Michael tightened his hold on her. "Not in this version, Cleo," he said with a sexy grin. One hand moved down to cradle her bottom and pull it into his growing erection. "In fact, I think things are just beginning to get interesting."

"So now we're making blue movies?" Cleo wasn't so sure she wanted to go this route, even if there wasn't a camera around to record their activities.

"No one is around. It's just you and me right now." He lifted her into his arms and headed for the nearby bed. When he got there, he laid her down gently and stretched out next to her. He grinned down at her. "I hope you don't mind, but I intend to make love to you every chance I get."

Parts of her thrilled at his bold declaration, but even so things were moving too fast for her. She pushed herself out of the bed, ignoring how her body protested the action. "I don't think I'm quite up for that just now, Michael."

He propped his head on his hand and stared at her. "Why should we deny ourselves, Cleo? You want me and I want you. So sex with me leads to feeding—there's nothing wrong with that."

There probably wasn't from his perspective. Michael was nonchalant about their having sex, even if she was a vampire and he a human. "It's just feels wrong, Michael. I don't want to use you that way."

"You aren't using me. I like feeding you and I really like having sex with you." He grinned at her. "How can that be anything but normal?"

"Michael, you have a distinctly weird view of normal."

He laughed out loud. "Why thank you! That could possibly be the nicest thing you've said about me."

Ignoring him for the moment, Cleo riffled through the pile of scripts, looking for something that would distract them both. "Here, why don't we try this one?"

Michael took it from her and if anything his grin grew broader. "Sure, Cleo. This will be great. We'll start at scene thirteen."

"Thirteen?" She thumbed through the pages until she got to the one he'd selected and realized why he was grinning. She started to back away from him. "Oh, no."

Michael was positively gleeful. "Oh, yes."

Of course. She would have to pick one of the scripts with a full-on actual love scene in it. Cleo began to back away. "Now, Michael, don't you think we should pace ourselves?"

He stalked after her, a determined smile on his face. "Pacing myself is just what I want to do."

"But I thought we were just supposed to be making movies."

From the doorway came a strange woman's voice. "Yeah, Michael. At least give us a chance to set up the cameras before you go at it."

With an audible groan, Michael came to a sudden halt. "Trust Tammy to show up on time for once," he muttered under his breath as a teenaged-looking girl with tawny hair entered the soundstage. Following her came a heavily bearded man who was a few years older. He wore a thin black tank top that exposed an amazing amount of dark curly hair on his chest and shoulders. Effortlessly the newcomer carried in several large metal cases that each made a heavy clunk when he lowered them onto the floor.

The young woman dropped her only slightly smaller load on top of his then grinned and snapped her gum loudly. "Did we interrupt something?" she said, and Cleo thought she sounded hopeful. Was this perhaps one of Michael's former conquests? She hoped not—the girl couldn't be much over eighteen.

"Not really," Michael said, but Cleo thought his voice sounded forced. He put his arm around Cleo and directed her to where the newcomers waited. "Cleo, I want you to meet some fellow parafolk. This is Tammy and George. They're here to help us set up some cameras and microphones so we can do some real screen tests."

Cleo held out her hand and it was caught in the surprisingly strong grip of first the man then the girl. "You're parafolk?" she asked, confused. Neither of the pair had obvious signs of being anything but normal outside of their strength. But maybe the cases weren't as heavy as they seemed.

Tammy's grin grew wider. "Yeah, we're both shapeshifters. Michael asked us to help you out making some films. I'm in film school, a sophomore this year at the university, but I've got nights off and want to study sound recording. George is a freelance cameraman."

"A shapeshifter?" Cleo asked in disbelief.

The young woman held out one hand and as Cleo watched in astonishment the fingers elongated and twisted into a paw, suddenly developing claws like those of a wolf. For an instant Cleo was reminded of the "dog" that had followed her the night before when she'd attempted to escape Michael and wondered if he'd had help in tracking her. Also there had been that young woman on the cell phone near the theatre. Had Cleo seen that particular golden-brown hair color before?

Oblivious to Cleo's thoughts, Tammy cracked her gum. "We've got a couple days before the full moon but the change is already starting for George so he had to call in sick to work this week. That makes him available for Michael to hire."

George rolled his eyes and shrugged. "I work at the big studios normally, but when I'm like this it's better to avoid notice, so I end up taking a few days off."

He gave a heavy, put-upon sigh. "Some of the guys have even taken to calling it my 'monthly', if you know what I mean. It's a real pain actually. Sure would be nice to work with my own kind so I wouldn't have to keep hiding."

The shapeshifter opened one of the cases, revealing what had to be a fifty-pound professional movie camera and lifted it from the box without straining a muscle. Meanwhile Tammy opened another case and pulled out a huge sound recording system, which Cleo knew had to weigh nearly as much as she did. The slender shapeshifter had no trouble carrying it into a quiet corner before plugging it in.

There really were such things as shapeshifters — which explained all the hair on George, Cleo thought. She tried to avoid letting her expression show just how astonished she was, but she felt Michael's amusement as he directed Tammy and George as to where to put the equipment.

When it was set up the way he wanted, Michael pulled another script off the pile. Cleo noticed the title — *Landscape of the Lost*, a low-budget dinosaur film with mostly grunting for dialogue, scanty costumes and not a single love scene.

He held it out to Cleo. "Let's try this one... The other one can wait until later. When we're alone," he added privately in a suggestive tone.

Cleo took the script and found an empty chair to sit in while she pretended to study it. She considered everything Michael had done to set up their situation. She was in a studio he'd gotten access to, studying a part in an old screenplay that he'd found copies of. Nearby was a professional cameraman that Michael had hired, setting up equipment he'd rented.

All of it seemed to be designed to give back her seventy-years-gone passion of making movies the way she had in her youth.

All of it was to convince her that having him as her companion was the best possible thing for her.

It was actually kind of scary—she was beginning to think he might have a point.

Chapter Seven

ಬಿ

It took about four hours to get scenes from both *Guns, not Roses* and the dinosaur movie, *Landscape of the Lost,* shot even with George's expert help. Cleo had forgotten what hard work filming could be and was exhausted by the time the last take had been declared.

Part of the problem was that Tammy apparently hadn't much experience handling a boom mike and several times she'd come close to hitting Cleo in the head. Even with Tammy's fervent "sorry"s Cleo wasn't completely sure that the near misses had been completely accidental, but she hadn't wanted to spoil things by making a scene.

Even tired and aching from the unaccustomed activity, it had been the most exciting evening she'd had in recent history, and that wasn't including making love with Michael earlier. Cleo was having fun.

Now the footage was in the can and Michael declared shooting over for the evening. After they'd finished filming, the shapeshifters didn't seem ready to leave and Cleo didn't know if she wanted to encourage that or not. Part of her wanted to be alone with Michael, but part of her was concerned about doing so.

It was something of a dilemma. So when Michael proposed watching a movie as an end to the night and both Tammy and George opted to stay, she'd decided to stay non-committal about their hanging around.

Without a word she followed as Michael led the way to the studio's screening room with a collection of DVDs in hand — old films, some of them obviously hers.

Michael seemed to be enjoying himself tremendously. As everyone selected beverages from a small refrigerator and found seats among the dozen or so couches and ancient padded armchairs, he pulled out a DVD copy of *Mate of the Monster*.

"Cleopatra is of the opinion that she's beyond acting now that she's a nightwalker. I think we need to remind her of just how great she was."

Cleo paused in mid-pour of her glass of icy cold serum. "I am not going to sit through a movie marathon of my old titles."

He held up the box with its distinctive cover of the barely clad blonde Cleo in the arms of a giant gorilla. "Just this one, Cleo."

From his seat in the front George lifted his beer bottle and took a hefty swig. "Wasn't Roger Dash the cinematographer on that? I've always wanted to see the camera work he did there...it broke new ground from what I heard." He gave Cleo a healthy look of respect. "What I saw in the camera tonight wasn't bad, but you must have been pretty good to work with the best in the business for a little horror film."

"She's still really good. That's what I'm trying to convince her," Michael said.

Still-under-twenty-one Tammy examined the diet cola Michael had given her with an audible sniff, apparently miffed she wasn't allowed anything stronger. "Sure, let's see the nightwalker in her prime. Maybe it will impress me."

Cleo knew that the young shapeshifter didn't like her very much. Not having had many friends during the past many years, the other woman's disdain didn't bother her much but it did make her wonder what she'd done to deserve it. She wasn't sure what she'd do about it if she did know, but she was curious. Maybe if Tammy hung around for the next few days she'd get a chance to find out.

Outvoted on the choice of movie, Cleo sat on one of the couches while Michael loaded the player in the back of the room. She regretted the larger seat when Michael returned to settle in next to her.

He grinned at her. "You don't mind sharing, do you?"

Her answer wasn't heard as the opening credit music suddenly blared from the room's excellent sound system. Resigned, Cleo sipped her serum and wondered if she shouldn't have laced it with vodka then cringed as the first shot of her bleached-blonde head filled the screen. Why had she let them change her hair color for this movie? She hated being a blonde.

As the movie progressed she became less self-conscious of her hair and more involved in the story. A relatively small-budget film of the time, it relied on careful camera angles, special lighting and strong acting to carry the story rather than expensive special effects. She remembered how often the director had regaled her to get the shot right the first time to avoid expensive reshoots.

Fortunately that hadn't been difficult. Most of what was in the movie had been the first or second take... She'd rarely had to do a third and almost never a fourth unless something else had gone wrong.

She'd been that good at getting it right most of the time. In Cleo a funny feeling rose...pride for what she'd been able to accomplish all those years ago.

Next to her Michael sighed and Cleo glanced over to see his face enraptured as the filmed Cleo opened her arms to her co-star in the film, the half-man, half-beast "monster" of the title.

In her mind came Michael's mental voice. *You were so beautiful, Cleo. Look how luminous you are.* Michael turned towards her and she could see his eyes in the light from the projector. *You're still that way. You light up on film as much now as you did then.*

In his eyes Cleo read some deep emotion, more than desire, more serious than lust. Admiration was there...but something more as well.

Love? Was it possible he cared that deeply for her? Disconcerted, Cleo tried to move away but his arm captured her, pulling her close.

I am so glad you are here, Cleo. You will see. It's going to be great.

What will be great?

She as much felt as heard his deep chuckle. *We'll be great. The studio will be great, the films we make will be great. And you and I...we'll be more than great together.*

His hand cupped her shoulder, caressing it, warm even through the fabric of her shirt. Shivers of excitement sped up and down her arm. *Have you ever made out in a movie theatre?*

She cast a quick glance at the shapeshifters, but all she could see were the backs of their heads. They were obviously engrossed in the movie.

In the film's story, Cleo's character redeemed a man so overcome by his beast-like nature that he had been magically transformed into a monster. Her gentle acceptance of him gradually turned him back into the man he used to be and eventually he remained that way. Cleo worried a little that the plot and its not-so-subtle anti-beast message might offend the shapeshifters, but instead they seemed to be enjoying it.

Meanwhile, Michael's hand had moved from her shoulder to her breast, and Cleo was enjoying that very much. Her breathing sped up as he flicked two talented fingers across her nipple, teasing it through the fabric.

From the front of the room she thought she saw Tammy's head tilt as if listening, and for an instant Cleo wondered how good shapeshifter hearing was. But then Michael's hand moved under her shirt and stroked her bare skin, teasing it to new levels of sensitivity, and Cleo decided not to care.

After all, their hearing couldn't be that good if Michael wasn't worried about them overhearing. Instead of worrying about the shapeshifters, she focused instead on how wonderful he made her feel.

With every scene they'd performed tonight, there had been a hint of sexual awareness of each other, and now that they no longer had an audience...or at least their audience was preoccupied elsewhere, Cleo felt compelled to act on it.

Apparently so did Michael. No longer interested in the film, Michael cupped and stroked her breast while his other hand slid slowly into the front of her pants. It paused to fondle her soft curls then one finger probed through the folds to find her clit, circling it with sly intent.

Cleo was barely able to contain her shriek as that most sensitive part of her woke to instant awareness.

Join minds with me, Cleo. That way I'll be able to help keep you quiet.

She should just tell him to keep his hands out of her pants and then she'd have no problem staying quiet. But, well...his finger felt so good. Even with their making love earlier, she couldn't help wanting more from him.

Opening her mind, she let Michael's strong control surround her even as his hand slid further between her legs.

His fingers teased and excited her clit and a mini-orgasm sped through her on the spot. In her mind she felt Michael's blueness speed into purple lust but he made no sound and with their joining neither did she.

The first climax ended but Michael's hand didn't stop. He stroked her again and again, his fingers now deep in her pussy. Heavy petting had never felt so good in the past.

Past? What past? Being with Michael wasn't anything like her sexual experiences of her foolish youth. Never had she had a lover so in tune with her body, anticipating what she needed to reach completion almost before she recognized it herself.

His fingers drove deeper, reaching for a spot along the inside wall and stopping when her mind's shriek told him he'd found it.

Oh. So that's what they call a G-spot!

In silence Cleo came again and again. With her mind joined to Michael's she realized he could sense just where she got the most enjoyment from his fingers and focus his attentions there. She'd never had a man so efficient in bringing her to pleasure. Every stroke was just right. In her mind Cleo screamed over and over again, the need to keep silent enhancing the experience.

She reached over to touch Michael and found him hard as a rock, his cock a solid rod inside his pants.

It had to be uncomfortable. Maybe she should reciprocate?

I'll survive, Cleo. His mental voice was insistent. *This is just for your benefit right now.*

Had any man been this considerate before? Cleo couldn't remember…but then she could barely remember her name. One thing for certain, she'd keep this memory forever, of Michael making love to her with his hands while their company watched her old movie.

She came one last time then drew away from Michael, mentally as well as physically. He didn't fight it but let her slip away, his mind still filled with desire but content for now. She sensed his satisfaction at what he'd accomplished, bringing her ecstasy when she'd least expected it. He'd enjoyed her climaxes nearly as much as she had. One hand returned to cupping her shoulder, keeping her in a one-armed embrace on the couch. *I did enjoy them, Cleo. Making you happy makes me happy.*

I owe you, Michael.

I'm not keeping score, Cleo. Neither should you. Of course, there is later…

Leaning her head against his shoulder, her body still aglow from multiple orgasms, Cleo relaxed against his arm, feeling his strength. For so long she'd felt completely alone in the world but she didn't feel that way now. She'd loved the way Michael had held her mind in his while he pleasured her and would always remember it.

With a happy sigh Cleo turned her attention back to the closing moments of the movie.

Cleo's glow warmed Michael clear to the heart. For the first time she'd given herself over to him completely, for a brief moment trusting him, and she'd been rewarded with a pleasure he doubted she'd ever known before. There had been too much surprise in her for it to be otherwise.

Now she relaxed in his arms as if they'd been together for years and not just a few days. The next time it would be easer to talk her into trusting him. That as much as anything else was the importance of this moment.

He could tell how rare this kind of feeling was for her, both the trust and the sexual satisfaction as a result. She'd been alone for far, far too long.

But she wasn't alone anymore. Now she had him and if he could win her trust permanently he would have her forever — which just might be long enough to satisfy him.

The movie ended and the shapeshifters rose to leave.

"I was right," George said. "There was a lot of great camera work. Excellent movie and you were terrific." He spoke courteously to Cleo, although there was a twinkle in his eye when he smiled.

"The sound was pretty good too," Tammy added. "And the lighting. I wonder if we could do something like that here. As for the acting…" A look of begrudging respect entered her face. "Okay, Cleo, I've got to admit, you were pretty good."

"I told you she was," Michael gloated.

Cleo thanked them and spent a few moments cleaning up the projection room while they got ready to leave. Michael busied himself with the equipment then left the room.

Just before heading for the exit, Tammy called to her and Cleo went over. While the shapeshifter's earlier animosity seemed to be tempered, there was still a lack of friendliness that made Cleo cautious.

"I guess you haven't been around a lot of shapeshifters, have you?" Tammy said.

"No, you're the first I've met."

Tammy grinned. "I thought so. Just thought you should know. I can hear a frightened bunny pant at fifty paces. Nice to discover that nightwalkers breathe fast sometimes too."

Cleo stiffened. In spite of their precautions Tammy and George had known what was going on in the back of the screening room. Michael must have known they would. And he'd embarrassed her that way… When she got her hands on him…

Tammy wasn't finished. "I've known Michael a long time. He's practically an uncle to me and has run interference for me with my dad lots of times. You see, I'm not exactly a model shapeshifter daughter — well, that's not important," she said with a shrug. "What is important is that Michael's special and I like him a lot."

The young shapeshifter narrowed her eyes. "I know you made him really upset when you ran out on him before — and Michael never gets upset about unimportant things. That means you're important to him and I think you could hurt him."

She glared at Cleo and bared her unusually straight but very pointed teeth. "So don't," she said menacingly.

Perplexed, Cleo stared at the young woman. "Don't what?"

"Don't hurt him. You do, you'll have to answer to me — and plenty of other parafolks. Michael's got a lot of friends."

This puppy was threatening her? Secretly amused, Cleo tried for nonchalance. "If he has so many friends why does he need me?"

Tammy shrugged. "Don't you watch the movies? Guys fall in love with the wrong women all the time."

Cleo's amusement left abruptly. Could it be possible? "Michael's not in love."

"Sure he is," Tammy said with a snort. "But even he doesn't know how much — at least not yet. So make sure you're right for him or I will make sure you don't hurt anyone again. No place you can hide from me, no place I can't follow." Under the thin tank top her small breasts lifted with pride. "I've done it before and I'll do it again."

She knew it! Michael had had her followed to the theatre by a shapeshifter. So much for the offer to give her a head start. He'd never intended to give her a chance to escape him and had stacked the deck against her from the beginning.

But the rest of what Tammy had said sunk home... He'd done it because he loved her? Cleo wasn't quite ready to take Tammy's word for that.

Tammy knew it too. "I can tell you don't believe me. Fine. Just remember that I'll be looking for you if you hurt him again."

She growled and looked as threatening as a young, short, female werewolf could look. Okay, maybe the kid didn't really look like a puppy, but the girl's display didn't impress Cleo. Even so, she tried not to let that show as the teenager left the studio, the older shapeshifter in tow. He'd probably overheard the whole thing and she could tell he was hiding a smile.

With Michael elsewhere in the building, that left Cleo alone in the studio and for a moment she considered leaving. Yeah, he'd booby-trapped the doors, but all she'd have to do would be to grab one of the tarps lying about and cover herself to get past Michael's light traps. Hell, if she wanted to, she could probably peel back part of the siding on the building and make her own door. Cleo looked up at the ceiling vents, which would be easily accessible if the moon was full and she could fly, but in the meantime she could simply use a ladder like the one against the opposite wall.

There were plenty of ways out of a studio like this. She'd spent enough time in similar places to know. She didn't really need to stay the full three days Michael had demanded. It wouldn't even be light for another two hours. She could leave and get home, or find a new safe house and have her bed and the rest of her furniture moved before he could stop her.

"Hey, Cleo, ready to make love again?" Michael's voice came from nearby. She turned to see him leaning against the doorway, all lean muscle, black T-shirt stretched tight across his chest, blue jeans stretched even tighter across the massive bulge in his crotch. Cleo's mouth watered at the sight. He smiled at her.

"Didn't you say you owed me?"

Well, who said she needed to go home today? She could spend the next two hours moving furniture and searching for a place Michael couldn't find her, or she could spend the time making love to him.

Making love suddenly seemed the much better choice.

Flashing her sultriest smile, Cleo walked slowly over to him. "I thought you said we weren't keeping score."

Michael leaned in to kiss her hard on the lips. "Only score I want to make tonight is with you. I've even got a special place in mind to do it."

Letting her weight fall into his arms, she smiled up at him. He lifted her effortlessly and proceeded to carry her from the room.

"I like the way you think, Michael," she said, wrapping her arms around his neck.

But she didn't always like the way he acted, she decided not two minutes later when he carried her through the door into his "special place".

Well, so much for moving her bed to a new safe house. Cleo stared at the centerpiece of the fantasy bedroom Michael had created—her grandmother's four-poster bed! For a moment she was struck dumb with astonishment then she turned what she hoped was a steely glare on him.

It must have been pretty steely. Michael actually blanched and set her onto her feet, stepping away from her.

"I thought I'd surprise you. You were thinking about your bed…"

She gave in to her outrage. "That didn't give you permission to move it from my home!"

"Home? Really, Cleo, did you really think of the place that way? I checked it out while you were hiding from me. There was no art on the walls, very few books or movies, hardly anything distinctive about the place. Outside of the bed which you'd set up in the walk-in closet, and a chair and TV in the living room, there weren't any furnishings in it at all." He waved his hand around, and she noticed that most of her meager belongings had also magically been transferred from the Santa Monica house that had sheltered them for so long.

"Since there was so little I thought you'd be more comfortable having your stuff here."

Cleo's heart sank. How was she going to get away now? Michael not only held herself captive but her belongings as well. She sat on the so familiar bed and tried not to give in to despair. No man had made her cry since Rodriquez and she wasn't going to be reduced to tears now.

"It may not have been much to you...but it was my home, Michael. No, I didn't have a lot in it. I couldn't afford much but I valued what I had." She picked up one of the pillows on the bed. The pillowcase was edged with embroidery that one of her great-aunts had made in the late eighteen hundreds. "It was my home and you took it apart as if it were nothing."

Michael took a seat in the rocking chair that had been in her living room, a troubled look on his face. He rubbed his jaw with his hand. "I guess this wasn't such a good idea. I thought you'd like having your own things around you. I hadn't thought about the way you'd take it."

He stared at the bed, a miserable look on his face. "You're right, Cleo. It was presumptuous. I should have asked you first."

She couldn't answer him. She knew he wasn't reading her mind, but it was as if he had, so close had he come to describing her feelings.

Michael rested his face on his chin for a moment, as if deep in thought. Then he nodded slowly. "Okay, I'll have everything moved back tomorrow."

He reached under the bed and pulled out a suitcase. "Here are your clothes. I had them brought for you."

She opened the case and saw a couple of outfits, including three pairs of underwear. Just three. The dresser that matched the bed was still back in her house with the rest of her clothing.

"You brought my bed but you didn't bring all my clothes?"

"I told you that I was only going to keep you for a couple of days, Cleo. I meant that. By the time you need more, we'll have settled this."

He really did intend to let her go if she stayed with him for the three days and bringing her bed here was simply to make her more comfortable. She gave him a long steady look, thinking about all the expenses he'd racked up so far. Renting the studio, equipment, hiring a cameraman and now this, moving her furniture. "How can you afford all this? It is pretty expensive to move stuff around this way."

Michael shrugged. "Money isn't a problem. I've got plenty."

Cleo blinked at him. "You have money? But I thought you wanted me to take care of you. You were living in your former master's house…"

For a moment Michael stared then he burst out laughing. "Is that what has you spooked—money? You thought I was going to move into your little place and you'd have to buy me groceries?"

Bewildered, Cleo stared at him. "Well, what else was I supposed to think? You said you wanted to be my companion and live with me. You were living in your former nightwalker's home."

"That's why you ran away, because you couldn't afford me? You meant financially because I didn't have my own home?" Some of his humor fled. "Come to think of it, that's pretty insulting."

He pulled a cell phone out of his jeans and hit some buttons. "Charlie? Yes—I know what time it is. Hell, you know what hours I keep. I need you to do me a favor and earn a nice fat commission. Remember that house we were talking about? The one overlooking the beach." He nodded. "That's the one. See what they'll take for it. We'll go over the paperwork this afternoon. Okay, talk to you then." He closed the phone and began to stalk towards her.

Cleo's jaw dropped. "You're buying a house in Los Angeles? Just like that?"

Michael paused in mid-stalk. "Lady Nightwalker, I have all the money I'll ever need…for me or anyone I care about. I could buy a dozen homes in Los Angeles if I needed them. But I don't. All I want is one home now so you don't think I'm a bum."

Her cheeks heated. "I don't think you're a bum."

"No, but I can see how you might have gotten the wrong idea. Charlie has been after me to buy a home of my own for years now. So now I've bought it. Overlooking the beach, closed garage, private pool, hot tub and lots of space. The master bedroom will be easy to day-proof for a nightwalker."

He moved slowly towards her again. "It's a great place. I've thought about buying before but could never build the enthusiasm to own my own home. Too much responsibility." A self-conscious laugh escaped him. "See, you're a good influence on me, making me into a respectable homeowner."

He stopped just inches from her, so close she could feel the heat come off his body. "It's a great place, but if you don't like it, I'll buy another and another and another until I find someplace you do like and are willing to live in. And then it will be up to you."

Nervously she licked her lips. "What will be up to me?"

He leaned forward, his lips poised to land on hers. "It will be your choice, Cleo, not only which house to live in but whether or not I live there too."

It was all she could do not to whisper. "My choice?"

His smile told her everything she wanted to know. "Your choice. Always." He looked longingly at the bed she sat on. "It is definitely your choice whether or not I stay with you now and share your bed when you go to sleep this morning. I want to do that, Cleo."

She hadn't slept with a human since her conversion and she hesitated to do it now. "I don't breathe when I sleep and I can't wake up. That's why people think a vampire is dead when they find them. I'm told it's creepy."

"You aren't the least bit creepy, Cleo, and I want to sleep with you. There isn't anything wrong with it. Nightwalkers sleep with their lovers all the time," his hand reached for her face and caressed her cheek. "I want to be your lover and that includes sharing your bed. Will you let me?"

He lifted her chin so her gaze met his, and she read the warm caring in his brown eyes. How could she say no? "I guess I do owe you," she said, using that as an excuse to give in to him.

"I said I wasn't keeping score. But if that gets me where I want to be…" His voice trailed off as his lips finally landed on hers, caressing them gently.

This wasn't a passion-ridden kiss, not hard and overwhelming as he'd kissed her earlier but soft and questioning. Questioning whether he was going to be allowed to proceed. Cleo knew he'd stop anytime she told him to.

He wouldn't want to, but she knew the edge was off their need for sex. The first time they'd made love they'd both been driven to couple as fast as possible. Cleo hadn't had a man since Rodriquez's death and she was pretty sure it had been the first time in a while for Michael. A fast and furious sex act had been the result.

But now things were more relaxed and they could take their time for leisurely lovemaking. Also, the first time had been on the cot in the studio and both had had to be careful not to roll onto the floor. Now they were able to stretch out across the bed and have space to work with.

Michael started by undressing her, slowly inching her shirt off over her head to again reveal her breasts to his greedy eyes. When they were bare he spent a long time playing with them, using his hands and mouth and enjoying the weight of her breasts as he massaged them. By the time he'd satisfied his desire for suckling her nipples, Cleo was writhing on the bed, her hands clutching at the bedcovers.

He slid his hand inside her jeans and found her clit, swollen and ready for his attention. This time though, he undid the closure and slid her pants down her hips, giving him better access. Again Cleo cried out at his touch and he didn't try to cover her mind with his to prevent it.

He spread her legs wide and used his tongue, lips and teeth on her clit and folds while his fingers delved deep into her pussy. With unerring accuracy he found her G-spot and pressed hard as he took a particularly strong suckle on her clit.

Cleo moaned and then screamed as an orgasm raced through her. Michael's greedy mouth lapped her pussy and caught her juices as they poured from inside her during her climax. When Michael sat back he licked his lips and his smile held smug male satisfaction.

Equally greedy, Cleo sat up and pulled his black T-shirt out of the top of his pants and slid it up over his chest, revealing his nipples and their outline of curly brown hair. Michael lay back on the bed and smiled as she explored his body, letting her fingers and tongue find those places he liked best to be stroked. Every time she found one he let out a little groan, his eyes closing in reaction.

She leaned over him. "Maybe I should give you a backrub this time?"

Michael opened his eyes. "I'm not sure I want to get that relaxed right now." He tugged on the buttons of his jeans, opening them and releasing his cock to wave in the air.

Cleo reached for it and stroked it with her hand but when she went to put it in her mouth Michael stopped her. "Not now," he said, holding her face with his hand. The expression on his face was wanting but resolute. "I can't let you go down on me unless…"

"Unless what?" To her surprise she found that she really wanted to give him oral sex and taste him again.

"Unless you give me new marks, right now. On my neck."

For a moment Cleo was actually tempted to do just that. After all, he was already marked and she could always remove them later.

But that might be dangerous. She only had his word that he would let her remove them. As far as she knew only the fact that he was too embarrassed to show anyone the ones she'd left before prevented him from forcing her to keep him as a companion.

Of course, she argued with herself, keeping him might not be as bad as she'd thought. She really had believed she'd be responsible for providing him a home and groceries and she couldn't have afforded that. Knowing Michael wasn't destitute and that he had his own source of funds did make a difference.

Not enough to give up her freedom, but it did make the situation more tempting. Even so, she had two more days until the full moon to make up her mind and she wasn't quite ready to quit yet.

She let go of his cock and wriggled out of her pants. "If you won't let me go down on you, I'll just have to do something else."

There was a hint of disappointment in his face, but Michael pulled off his own jeans and dropped them on the floor. "What do you have in mind?" he asked when he was finally naked.

She pulled back the covers, revealing the soft cotton sheets she insisted on keeping on her bed. Since all she'd done in the bed was sleep instead of using it for sex, Cleo had grown used to making comfort rather than appearance her number one priority.

For the first time though, she wondered how black satin might be to sleep on. Slippery, she expected, but it would hide bloodstains.

"Lie on the bed, Michael."

"You going to give me a backrub after all?" he asked as he obeyed, lying on his stomach.

"No. Lie on your back. I'm going to give you a front rub."

"I told you…" he started to warn her.

Cleo shook her head. "You really need to trust me at least a little. My mouth isn't going anywhere near your cock."

"Okay—" he seemed skeptical as he turned over, exposing his lovely erection to her again.

Cleo straddled his hips and let her folds rest against him. Then she rubbed herself along his shaft, a single long stroke that made him gasp. Michael stared up at her as she repeated the action then smiled broadly, eyes bright with excitement. "That's pretty interesting."

It was for her as well. After Michael's attentions earlier her clit was fully erect and her pussy wept with natural lubricant, making her slide along his cock a delight. Each stroke rubbed her clit along his cock, sending frissons of pleasure into her.

There was also something satisfactory about being in charge of giving him pleasure this once. After their encounter in the screening room, it felt good to make him groan aloud.

But that reminded her... Cleo leaned over Michael, now clutching her hips and helping to direct her stroke. "There is something we should discuss."

"Could we do it later?" he gasped, his eyes shut with pleasure.

"It has to do with shapeshifter hearing and how good it is."

Michael's eyes snapped open and turned cautious. "Oh. I was going to tell you about that."

Now that she had his attention, Cleo stilled her hips and refused to move. "Any particular reason you wanted to embarrass me like that?"

"That wasn't it." He looked increasingly anxious for her to continue her "front rub" but she wasn't moving until he explained.

Michael sighed. "Shapeshifters are very territorial and don't always trust nightwalkers. There have been problems in the past...but you don't need to know about that now. What I needed to do was establish that there was a relationship between us so they would accept you as mine.

Without a mark in an obvious place what we did was the best way to show it."

"Why not just fuck me in front of them?"

He winced at her coarse language. "It didn't need to go that far. At first I was just going to make out a little with you, but things got carried away. George wouldn't have told you so I suppose Tammy did," he said with a grimace. "I'll get that little pup for that. I'm sorry you were embarrassed. That wasn't my intention."

There was so much about parafolk she didn't understand, but this did give her another explanation for Tammy's antipathy. She'd thought the shapeshifter had a crush on Michael, but it was her being a nightwalker that was the issue.

There had been problems in the past between shapeshifters and nightwalkers — she could only imagine what that meant. How was she ever going to fit into this new world when she didn't even know who might be her friend or her enemy? At this point the only person she could count on was Michael, who had kidnapped her and was forcing her to stay with him.

His cock twitched underneath her, making her clit ache for more action. Okay, so forced was probably the wrong word at this point. She was more than willing to make love with him.

As he continued to look at her anxiously, it occurred to her that she was still the one in control. He'd made it her choice, only asking her to give him the chance to prove himself. He'd sworn to let her go if she wanted, which was more choice than Rodriquez had given her.

"I think I understand, Michael. The next time you might explain first what's going on."

With a look of relief he nodded, and she shifted her hips again, driving their bodies together. Michael clutched her ass with both hands and went back to making low groans with each stroke of her body against his. This time she didn't stop until he grabbed her waist to slow her down. "Please, Cleo. I want to be inside you."

She wanted him there as well. Her body ached for his cock in her. Lifting her hips, she used her hand to raise his cock to meet the entrance to her pussy and sat down, sliding him deep within her.

Michael groaned appreciatively and Cleo couldn't help her own moan of satisfaction. It felt too damn good. She rose and sat again, milking him with her pussy. He grabbed her waist, holding on but not directing her, his hands firm but gentle.

That was something else she'd noticed. Whenever Michael touched her there was gentleness and Cleo felt cherished by the way he held her. She rose and fell on him, and he lifted his hips with each stroke, turning her efforts to make love to him into a joining of equal partners.

Just as their bodies were joined, she felt his mind slide against hers, blue streaked with purple. As she had earlier, she invited him in to share his passion with her and their minds mingled together, blue-purple with her gold. Bloodlust rose as well and she leaned into his chest, the only part of him she could easily reach. The vein there was harder to find but she managed, biting deep. Michael jerked but made no protest and in her mind she felt his acceptance of her need for his blood. Even so, he controlled her feeding, only letting her drink enough to take the edge off. She was so close to orgasm already it was easy for her to break off and erase the wounds as the first crest of climax rose in her.

Orgasms hit her in waves this time, the first climax hard, the second harder, and by the third Michael was also coming, his body jerking beneath her as she continued to ride his cock. Deep inside her she felt his cock shudder and release his cum, pulsating and hot, spurring her into a fourth mind-bending climax.

Having experienced the melding of their minds twice now, it was easier for her to stay joined this time. Michael's and her mental voices seem to cry out in unison with their physical counterparts as shared passion exploded in them both.

In the aftermath Cleo felt a little lost. So many thoughts and emotions swirling around, some hers, mostly his, and she let her mind slide away to the safety of her own head. She felt his disappointment as she split away but it wasn't as profound as it had been earlier. At least this time she'd stayed with him through their climax and from his smile that had been enough to make him happy.

Later, sated and sleepy, Cleo lay with Michael in her grandmother's bed and acknowledged to herself that it really was better sharing a bed with another person. Waiting for the dawn, she relaxed in a lover's arms for the first time since Rodriquez had died. For seventy years she'd told herself she didn't mind being alone at the break of dawn when sleep stole over her and left her helpless.

She'd lied. With Michael she felt secure and protected. Another new memory—lying in someone's arms when she fell asleep.

In her mind came Michael's mental voice. She felt as much as heard his weariness. *I've never actually slept with a nightwalker before.* He kissed the back of her neck. *It's nice.*

I haven't slept with a human…

A companion, he corrected her.

A companion, then. Sorry. I haven't slept with anyone since…

She'd thought she'd cut off the completion of that thought soon enough, but Michael startled and weariness seemed to fall away from him. "Rodriquez? Emmanuel Rodriquez? Was he your maker?"

It was too close to dawn now for her to speak aloud. Cleo let her mind nod her answer.

The next thing she heard was Michael sputtering, swearing, then "Well, no wonder..."

Rest well, Michael. Cleo sent the thought into his mind before she could fall asleep.

Michael left off fuming aloud and his arms tightened around her. Through his gentleness she could still feel his fury.

You rest well, my Lady Nightwalker, and never fear. I will keep you safe.

Chapter Eight

ഇ

"I'm surprised you even know who he was. When I met him he was something of a recluse," Cleo said the following evening.

"Of course I know of him," Michael replied. "All parafolk do." Doing his best to control how upset he still was from her revelations the night before, he helped Cleo select costumes from the studio's abandoned costume bank for the evening's filming. It was normally impolite to make disparaging comments about a nightwalker's maker, and he didn't want to offend Cleo.

Still, it really was hard to not say how much he despised Rodriquez. He'd heard too many stories about the nightwalker.

"What do you know about him?"

Michael considered saying nothing but decided someone would tell her soon enough. It might as well be him.

"He was a renegade. Made up his own rules and wouldn't follow those of others. Some of the things he did...well, they got the rest of us in trouble and for that he was kicked out of parafolk society."

Interestingly, that didn't surprise her. Most likely she'd already known some of it. After all, she'd lived with the man.

"That explains why we were all alone. He told me there were no others like us around and I guess for him that was true." She held up a simple white gown. "You think this would do for the medieval story?"

She seemed to be taking this really well. Either that or she really didn't want to talk about her maker. Either way was fine with him. "I think it would be great."

Cleo smiled at him and pulled a tunic and tight pants off the shelf. "These would work for your part."

"Oh, no. I'm not wearing tights."

She fluttered her eyelashes at him. "Oh, but you'll look so dashing in them. You have really great legs, you know."

"I do?" He growled in return, feeling himself giving in.

"Oh yes…I can't wait to see you in them. And they'll look so good on camera."

Michael held out his arms and let her pile the offending clothing in them. He'd spent the afternoon with Charlie, the real estate agent, going over the paperwork for the house he wanted. They'd even set up closing for a week from now so he'd be able to move in before Vlad and Sam got back from their honeymoon.

So much paperwork to sign to buy a house, even outright from the funds of the dummy corporation he'd set to manage his finances. His hand still felt cramped from signing his name so many times. But he had a house now, a nice one to offer Cleo. Once she saw it, he knew she'd love it, but if she didn't, he'd find another place and go though the whole thing again, no matter how bad his hand hurt.

About that point he realized he'd do anything for Cleo. Even wear tights.

With one last roll of his eyes he followed the slender figure out of the costume bank. It was far too late for caution. He was well and truly hooked.

Cleo stared at the iron manacles on her wrists, which held her arms to the wall above her head. "Are you sure these things are necessary? I thought the heroine was simply tied in the script."

The screenplay tonight was a costume drama about medieval times with castles, swords and elaborate dialogue. Cleo hadn't performed in one of those during her career and she was looking forward to it. At the very least the costume, a long, flowing white gown with an elaborate bodice that she looked stunning in, was worth the effort.

The plot featured a beautiful maiden, beloved by a poor but noble knight, who falls into the hands of a wicked Lord Havamore who wants her for himself. He imprisons her in a tower cell and threatens her lover's life unless she allows him to have his wicked way with her—that being the scene they were about to work on.

Dressed in her gown, Cleo was playing the lovely maid Alison while Michael was doing double duty, performing both the roles of villain and the hero, Sir Rodney, complete with tights.

After consulting the pages in front of him, Michael shrugged. "It says ropes, but I'd rather use chains. They're better visually."

"Oh." She gave them an experimental yank and was gratified to see one of the links open a little. As a nightwalker, only silver chains or the silver core ropes he'd used before could really hold her. That was something Michael was surely aware of.

She tugged again. Just a little more and she could be free…but she wouldn't do that right now. Michael apparently wanted her to pretend to be chained up or he'd have used the ropes. If Michael wanted to pretend she was incapacitated then she would play along.

It could even be fun to see how far he planned on carrying this. Her first read of the script had revealed an intriguing sexual plotline where the bound heroine tries to trick her wicked captor into releasing her, wielding her femininity like a sharpened sword. With Michael the potential object for her charms, it was possible events could go quite differently from the printed page.

In Cleo's opinion this was one script where the villain was far more interesting than the hero. She had great hopes for the scene and since in real life vampires rarely got a chance to play the part of a submissive, she was curious as to how that would work out. Okay, more than curious.

Letting Michael dominate her sounded like a whole lot of sensual fun.

Cleo hid her grin as Michael advanced on her with the script in hand. "The scene is a pivotal one for you. You have no idea that the hero is about to arrive on the scene so put everything you have into trying to seduce the bad guy."

She nodded, keeping her face as straight as possible. "Put everything into seducing the bad guy. Will do."

Caught off guard, Michael gave her a suspicious look but turned his attention to one last check of the lights and the camera setup. She'd told him the shapeshifters had phoned to say they would be late tonight, but Michael had decided to proceed anyway.

Cleo couldn't help her smile of satisfaction over that. George and Tammy had called while Michael wasn't around and she'd convinced them that they wouldn't be needed until much later. She doubted they would show up before this scene was well and truly over — one way or another.

Having Tammy or even George around didn't fit in with her vision of how the scene was going to go. Without the shapeshifters they were going to record the scene using two cameras with a wide focus. If the footage was good, then they'd shoot close-ups later. Secretly Cleo hoped to derail the scene to the point that Michael would never let the footage be seen any place else.

When he was finished with the cameras he returned to her. "Ready to begin?"

Stretching, Cleo let the chains clank together, reminding him of her position. The action also stretched tight the one-size-too-small white gown she'd selected for her costume. When she lifted her shoulders her breasts nearly popped out of the top of the gown.

Michael made a small noise deep in his throat and paused to adjust his tights, which, as Cleo'd predicted, looked fabulous on him. Stealing a glance at Michael's crotch, Cleo noted with satisfaction that he'd developed quite a bulge already. This was definitely going to be fun.

"Ready when you are," she said with a grin, not caring that he saw her fangs.

Again Michael cleared his throat and actually looked uneasy. Quickly Cleo suppressed her grin. No point in giving away the game too soon.

He looked through the script and found his first line as the evil Lord Havamore. "And so, my dear lady, you see you are in my power."

Throwing herself into the part, Cleo gave a realistic sigh of despair. "That I am, my lord."

"Lord Havamore" narrowed his eyes. "You understand I can do anything I want with you. There will be no rescue for you this time. No one knows you are here and by the time they do it will be too late." He leaned forward and leered into her face. "I will possess you, my lady."

Cleo feigned alarm. "But I am untouched, sir. Surely you would not besmirch me this way. I would not go to my wedding bed unchaste."

"Since I intend to make your wedding bed mine as well, it matters not how chaste you are when you get there. I would have a lust-loving wench in my bed, not a frightened virgin."

More and more Cleo was beginning to like this Lord Havamore. He had the right attitude about sex. Still she had to keep acting the part of the frightened virgin. She cringed away from him. "Oh please, good sir. Must you torment me with threats like these?"

"These are not threats, my lady. They are promises. I will have you...in fact, I could have you right now." He slid his hand down her cheek to her neck. "You are in no position to stop me."

Michael's hand gently caressed the swell of her breasts poking above her bodice. "You have a body made for lust, m'lady. Aren't you even the least bit curious as to the joining of man to woman? There are pleasures I could show you..."

Oh, and he could too. It was getting harder and harder to stay in character as the virginal Alison. Cleo found herself wanting to lean into that wayward hand of Michael's rather than shy away from it.

Fortunately this was where the script allowed her to act on her first choice. The intrepid Lady Alison was supposed to feign interest in the evil lord's plan and nearly seduce him before knocking him unconscious and escaping the tower to fly into the welcoming arms of her noble sweetheart.

At least that's what the script said. What Michael didn't know is that she had no intention of escaping from either the tower or the evil lord's clutches.

Now she leaned into him, as if her character had suddenly decided to play along with her captor. "Pleasures? Oh, my lord. What is it you speak of? I've never heard of there being pleasure in the interaction of man to maid. Is it kissing you refer to?"

She tried her patentable maidenly blush, last used in her role in *A Lady of Mischief*. "I do know that kissing can be a pleasant thing."

Michael's Lord Havamore looked ready to swallow his tongue. "Indeed. It can. Would you like me to show you just how pleasurable it is?"

Without waiting for a reply, he put his hands on the stone to either side of her, trapping her against the wall she was already chained to. With one motion he dipped his head to meet her lips. As soon as they touched, she opened her mouth and gave his tongue access and in no time Michael was taking full advantage of that, kissing her in a most non-heroic fashion, all tongue and teeth rather than a chaste placement of his lips on hers.

Non-heroic, but it was terrific nonetheless. As Cleo had suspected, the medieval rogue really was more fun than the proper knight. Her tongue met his in a fervent battle that left both of them gasping for air.

Michael leaned back, stared at her and dropped character. "I'm not so sure you should be kissing me, Cleo."

She tried her most innocent look. "But Lady Alison is trying to seduce him. Surely she'd kiss back."

Michael looked uncertain, but he nodded. "Okay, so we'll play the scene as if she means it." He took a heavy breath. "So where were we?"

Cleo dropped back into the character of Lady Alison. "Oh, m'lord. Your kisses are unlike anything I've ever known."

Michael grabbed his crotch meaningfully. "If you think my kisses are something, you won't believe my rod of manhood. I've brought women more experienced than you to tears of joy with my prowess."

"I'm sure tears of any other kind would be wrong. Please, good sir. Your kisses have made my body hot. Perhaps you could cool it down."

With a realistic leer, Michael seized the top of her gown. "Taking your top down would help, I'm sure." The script called for him to reveal just a hint more of her breasts, but to his surprise, the bodice came away easily in his hand, thanks to the earlier efforts of Cleo's scissors carefully snipping the seams so they ripped apart without damage.

As the front fell away, Michael was left gaping at Cleo's naked breasts. For a moment he stared at the bodice front in his hand. "I believe what we have here is a carefully prepared wardrobe malfunction."

Cleo shimmied against the faux stone wall, her full and very bare breasts rising up and down, recapturing Michael's attention. "I thought the scene needed some jazzing up. A little bodice ripping is quite in character for Lord Havamore."

Michael's lips twitched into a smile. "Hmm, you may have a point. Okay, let's see just how far this is going to go." He tossed away the bit of fabric and reached for the chains. "I'll just unfasten you."

"Is that what Lord Havamore would do?"

Michael seemed to consider that and his hand paused. "No." Redirected, his hand landed on her breast, tweaking the nipple gently. Cleo gave a moan that wasn't the least bit acting. Michael nodded. "So you want to do something naughty, Cleo?"

"Don't you mean Lady Alison, m'lord? And what do you mean by naughty?"

A totally wicked look took over Michael's face. "I mean, Lady Alison, that perhaps I should be concerned you might hit me over the head if you got your hands free." He tweaked her nipple again and she gave another non-acting moan.

"So, perhaps I should keep you bound a while longer. Now you are completely in my power and I think I should show you just what that means."

He lowered his face to her breasts and Cleo immediately understood what Michael meant by naughty. "Oh, my LORD!" she gasped as Michael proceeded to use his mouth tongue and teeth on her breasts with good effect. He nipped first one nipple then the other, swirling his tongue around the areola until Cleo was nearly hanging in her chains, her knees barely able to support her.

With a jerk, Michael lifted her against the wall, pulling her skirt up to rest around her waist and baring her. Hoping for just this situation, as well as working with what she knew was historical accuracy, Cleo had forgone wearing underwear and so Michael found no impediment to his questing hands.

Pausing for a wicked laugh that sent shudders of desire through her, he lost no time in sliding one finger in between her naked thighs to find her clit and circle it with evil intent.

If Cleo thought she'd been in heaven before, now she was over the moon. With his thumb still on her clit, he drove his long fingers further back to find her vagina and slid them in deeply, finding her G-spot again with unerring accuracy. He fingered her until she was gasping for breath against the wall behind her.

"You see, Lady Alison, that a man who knows what he's doing can be far more interesting than a fumbling boy. Be glad your virginity is going to me and not that fool Rodney."

"Oh, I am," Cleo panted. "Very glad. Show me more of the ways of men and women."

"Indeed I shall, for I will taste your honey now and in doing so prepare you for our joining."

Her eyes opened wide in mock surprise. "Taste me? But you have already kissed my lips."

"It is not the lips on your face I intend to savor but those between your shapely thighs." He licked his lips with anticipation.

"Oh surely that is an evil deed, m'lord!" Cleo cried.

"I will let you judge its evilness." Michael dropped to his knees and lifted her legs to balance across his shoulders, exposing her open pussy to his greedy mouth. He sucked hard on her clit, already sensitive from his earlier attentions, and she shrieked with pleasure.

"That must be a sin to feel so good," she said when she found her voice.

"What would be sinful would be to waste any of your sweetness," Michael told her. Then he pulled her closer and ran his tongue along her nether lips, taking time to lick her, nibble her and then push his tongue deep into her pussy. If she had been a virgin his wicked tongue could almost have deflowered here as it entered her so forcefully.

Tingles from his mouth's actions in her pussy sped into in her fingertips and down to the ends of her toes. Each lick of his tongue caused another frisson to run through her until she was near senseless.

When she was limp, he lowered her off his shoulders and stood supporting her against the wall.

"And now, my Lady Alison, I will make you mine in truth."

Michael pulled down his tights, revealing his erect cock. "What do you say, m'lady? Does this impress you?"

Cleo attempted to look quailed instead of drooling over Michael's sizable staff. "Impress and terrify, m'lord. Why, you will damage me with that thing!"

"'T'will only hurt for a moment. Then you will experience true ecstasy."

"Are you so certain, m'lord?"

"Aye, most certain, lass," Michael said, his character's voice momentarily slipping from wicked medieval lord into a Scottish brogue for a moment. Then he remembered who he was supposed to be.

"That is, I'm quite certain, m'lady. No woman has died in my bed from the size and breadth of my staff, or the way I've used it." He leaned in closer, rubbing his cock against her most intimate place. "At least they've not died in any sense but that of *la petite mort* — the little death."

Cleo's swoon was only partly pretend. "The little death? That sounds so ominous. But oh, m'lord, I'm not certain I can stand much more of this!"

"Then I will take away your need to stand at all." Having completely forgotten that the cameras were still running, Michael lifted Cleo against the wall and with one swift movement speared her pussy with his mighty shaft.

For a brief moment Cleo remembered the couple outside the club where she'd first met Michael, fucking against the alley wall. Then she'd been surprised at the man's strength, but her man was just as strong as he held her legs and wrapped them around his thighs.

Impressed and impaled, Cleo stared at him. "Michael…" she whispered.

He narrowed his twinkling eyes at her. "Don't you mean Lord Havamore?"

Michael thrust deep into her, withdrew and repeated. He then set up a rhythm of thrusts, holding her against the wall and driving home inside her with a ferocity that burned through her. Not able to move, unable to do more than accept his wild possession of her, Cleo gave herself over to him, his cock and the sensations that rose in her, sending her quickly into one orgasm after another.

"Oh, Lord Havamore!" Cleo exclaimed, lifting her legs higher to tighten around his waist. Straining against the shackles binding her to the wall, she pulled hard and the link she'd weakened earlier gave up. Cleo's arms fell away from the wall and onto Michael's shoulders, the falling chains barely missing his head.

He paid no attention, far too concerned with fucking than to worry about nearly being brained. As Cleo wrapped her arms around his neck, he jerked once, twice and in Cleo's mind she felt the purple of his passion.

Bloodlust rose and she bit into his neck, catching the vein and sucking hard. She drank until his mind overcame hers, the blue-purple haze filling her as much as his cock filled her pussy. Halted in her feeding, she released his neck and erased the wounds, her bloodlust sated once more.

She felt his mind blank out just as his peak hit and then all was confusion and blue-purple sparks as he came deep inside her. Cleo's mind was swept away with his, and she experienced both his orgasm and hers. Shuddering, she clung to him like a lifeline.

Recovery came slowly but when at last the tremors stopped they'd fallen to their knees on the floor and Michael was cradling her close. Covering her mind was his, all warm purple-blue passion.

If she hadn't already been told he loved her, she would have known it then. She could feel love pouring out of him. It was wonderful.

It was also frightening. It was true—Michael was in love with her. He'd promised to let her go if she didn't want to stay with him, but there was no way he was going to let her go.

But was that really a problem? Did she want to leave anymore? Her mouth was filled with the taste of his blood, her body still impaled by his cock, her mind comforted by the companionship of his. Michael was all things to her.

Maybe this wasn't such a bad thing after all.

Chapter Nine

ഇ

Cleo woke in Michael's arms…this was their third night and their last if she didn't agree to make him her permanent companion. When she woke, though, that wasn't the first thing on her mind.

The first thing she thought of was how warm and safe she felt. The second was that she was hungry and her dinner smelled wonderful.

The third thing was that her dinner also had a lusciously big erection lying along the cleft of her ass. It was hard to pick which of these events were most interesting. All had their own appeal. Fortunately, she didn't have to choose.

Michael felt her stir and flipped her to lie underneath him. "Good evening, my Lady Nightwalker," he said with a warm loving smile.

She returned his smile. "Good evening, Michael."

"Do you want to eat first then make love, or do it the other way around?"

Cleo forced herself not to laugh and instead pretended to seriously consider the question. "Why can't we make love while I eat?" Practically every time they made love she ended up taking some of his blood, usually not very much, but enough to keep her stomach happy. Somehow even a small amount of his blood satisfied her. She'd worried about feeding during sex but Michael had reassured her that it was perfectly normal and that he even found the pinpricks of her teeth erotic.

"There is a certain efficiency in that." Michael's smile turned sensual, a signal that turned Cleo's desire up to full force. In just the short time they'd been together, they'd found what drove each other into mind-bending arousal.

Outside of just their being together. That seemed to be sufficient most of the time anyway.

Less and less Cleo thought of how she was going to get away from him and more about how much she wanted to be with him. Even if he never said the words, she knew how much he cared for her. How much did she care for him? She dared not think too hard about that.

Never had a man affected her this way, not even when she'd been very young and more than a little foolish over one man or another. Men had come and gone, staying in her life for a while until one or the other of them had grown bored and moved on. Back then she'd had crushes, forever falling in love with someone, her heartthrob of the year, or month…or even week. Even Rodriquez had qualified at one point.

What she felt for Michael was different. This felt…real. And real wasn't something she was used to. It confused her.

But it was also wonderful and it made her happy in ways she couldn't express, at least not in words. She couldn't tell Michael, at least not yet. The best she could do was to show him how she felt.

She would make love to him. Real love because that's really what she felt…and Michael felt the same thing.

Cleo used some of her strength to push him over onto his back. He went willingly, not fighting her, letting her climb on top of him, letting her have her way for once. Michael smiled up at her, a hint of triumph in his face. He knew, she realized, just how close she was coming to seeing things his way.

He wanted to be her companion and the price was the same as it had always been, to give up her autonomy and live with Michael at her side. He'd answered her concerns about what they would live on and where they would stay. He'd shown her pictures of the new house and she could almost see herself living there.

In fact it was starting to sound pretty good. But what was really sounding good at the moment was a little female dominative sex, with her controlling him for a change.

If that's what you want, Cleo my Lady Nightwalker. Speaking mentally, Michael relaxed against the pillow, keeping his arms at his side. *I await your pleasure.*

Once again he'd been reading her thoughts and it gave her pause. Did she really want to be with someone from whom she could keep no secrets?

Michael read her hesitation. "I'm sorry, Cleo. It isn't that I mean to intrude. But sometimes you are so easy to read, particularly when I want so much to understand you."

He laughed, but the sound held the edge of bitterness. "Do you realize how little I know about you? You've told me barely anything at all and have fought to keep me out of your mind and life. Even so, I know you care about me, and that you know just how much I care for you."

He swallowed hard and Cleo could feel his concern about revealing so much of himself. "I've never said this to anyone. But Cleopatra Lutz—I love you."

Her heart just about leapt from her chest. "You love me?"

"I was infatuated with you when I was a boy, but I haven't been a boy for a very long time. I'm a grown man, ready for grown-up love and that's more than just sex, fun though that can be. It isn't like I've not had women before but with you it's all new again. Sex with you isn't just sex."

Before he could say more, Cleo silenced him by putting her finger over his mouth. "It isn't just sex with me either."

She stopped and let out a long breath. "I know what you want to hear...I'm not quite ready to say it yet."

His face lit up like a full moon. "You are thinking about it though."

"I think about little else." She leaned over him. "But thinking too much isn't what I need right now. I need to make love, Michael. I want you."

With a magnanimous smile, Michael stretched out beneath her. His cock rose large and full into the crotch of her legs, involuntarily stroking her most sensitive place. Cleo couldn't resist her low moan at the sensation.

Michael smiled at her reaction. "Whatever my Lady Nightwalker needs or wants, I'll be pleased to deliver. Just ask, Cleo. What you want is yours."

She leaned closer, letting her fangs graze his neck. Between her legs dampness grew, her pussy weeping all over his cock. As the warm dampness covered him, Michael's eyes closed and his breathing deepened. He rubbed himself against her, spreading her arousal along the length of his cock. Now both of them breathed heavily.

He felt too good. He smelled too good. She licked him and his taste drove her to distraction. Overcome, Cleo bit into his neck, letting his hot blood flow into her mouth.

Michael gasped but with one swift movement he directed his cock into her, spearing her to the hilt, his way eased by their mutual fluids. He lifted his hips to stroke deep within her and Cleo groaned aloud at his intimate invasion. She lifted herself over him and soon they were moving together. She'd thought she'd be in charge but she wasn't...they moved together as one, their bodies merging to their combined pleasure.

Their minds merged as well, blue-purple and gold into a composite that was all three colors. Then the colors seemed to heat, meld together into a single white-hot mass as they moved, Michael shifting his hips on the bed in a twisting motion that drove her beyond distraction.

Cleo took several long sips before she couldn't stay focused on eating any longer. Erasing the marks, she freed her mouth to cry out Michael's name, her orgasm instant and unrelenting. Michael too lost control and in an instant they'd both come, their thoughts and emotions so blended they couldn't tell one from another. She collapsed against him, his arms holding her close to him.

In the aftermath Cleo laid across him with her body shaking from their lovemaking. Lifting her head, she stared into his eyes, her emotions bound up with his. Their minds were still linked, the pair of them too overcome by the experience to pull away from the other.

Feeling exposed, she tried to pull away before he could stop her. Their minds parted abruptly but for once she didn't feel his dismay at their separation.

Michael lifted his hand to her cheek and smiled. "It's all right, Cleo. You can take your time."

"Time?" she said, confused. "Time for what?"

He took a deep breath. "I understand you aren't comfortable with the link. That's why you break it whenever it lingers past our making love. But it's all right. I know how new this all is for you." There was a touch of self-consciousness in his laugh. "The truth be told, I'm not all that comfortable with it myself. I want it…I know what it means that we can link like that and I welcome it but it does take some getting used to. Eventually we'll both learn to appreciate it."

Cleo watched him rise and find fresh clothes from his suitcase in the corner before going to the one he'd packed for her with items from her home. He'd remembered everything she'd need for the three days with him, including an extra pair of underwear...just in case she'd decide to stay with him longer.

That last pair was sitting in the bottom of the case, a reminder that tomorrow she'd be free. Or she'd be with him, looking over the new house he'd bought.

She still hadn't made up her mind which way to go. But she was starting to lean in a particular direction—one she suspected would make him very happy.

* * * * *

On the soundstage, they sat in folding chairs and read like an old married couple might do on a quiet evening. While Michael sorted through his pile of scripts, Cleo perused one of the trade magazines, catching up on the latest gossip.

He took special care in looking over the possible selections. This was their last night in the studio and he wanted something special. He'd secretly reviewed the footage he'd gotten from the "off-hours" shooting when the shapeshifters hadn't been around and it had been just Cleo and himself.

Wonderful stuff, powerful and sexy. Several times the scene they'd filmed had turned erotic, with Cleo or him initiating some act of intimacy and recording it for all time. He didn't think he would ever forget these moments alone with her but he loved having those memories on film, preserved for all time.

As glorious as Cleo looked normally on film, when it came to sex scenes she became luminous. In today's films, with their more explicit nature, she'd be a natural. Not that he'd encourage anything like that for her or show any of that secret footage to anyone but Cleo herself. Some things a man wanted to keep to himself, like his woman and his making love to her.

Even so, it had been illuminating watching. As he viewed the footage in the order it had been shot, he'd noticed how Cleo changed with time. At first she'd been reserved, almost shy, as if terrified of stepping into the limelight that had once been her domain. But she'd rediscovered herself during their filming and grown bolder. In particular the medieval seduction scene had been wonderfully sexy and a lot of fun.

He'd laughed and gotten hard at the same time but he'd also realized just how far she'd come in the three days she'd been with him.

Since tonight was the full moon and their film crew was off doing shapeshifter things, he wanted to do something special for their last film excerpt...something very erotic. Something intense, arousing and appropriate for a man to act out with the woman he loved—a memory to put on film and keep forever.

He lifted one of the scripts, a western...no, too much sun-baked sand. Michael tossed it to the side. He didn't want Cleo remembering why she no longer saw herself as an actress unable to work in the day.

Cleo frowned at her magazine. "It says here that there was a movie shot on a single soundstage and they used digital effects to put in everything around the actors, including crowds, the sky and landscape." She laughed. "We used to do that all the time in the old days...it just didn't look very good."

With a critical eye she examined the photographs in the article and nodded approvingly. "These look real. You know, we could do that. Shoot a beach movie at night on a soundstage and add the ocean and sun in later."

She grinned at him, letting the tips of her fangs show. "Imagine me in a bikini!"

Oh, he could. Michael closed his eyes for a moment to do just that and his cock turned hard again, even though they'd just gotten through making love not an hour before. Cleo dressed in a miniature swimsuit. Maybe something with tiger stripes…or tie-dyed to contrast with her ultra-pale skin.

"Have you decided what we're doing tonight?" Cleo's voice broke through his fantasies of tiny strips of fabric tied across her luscious flesh. He returned to his examination of the rest of his pile.

"No, not yet. I'm looking for something special…"

And just like that he found it. Resisting the urge to shout "Eureka!" and dance around the soundstage, Michael held onto the dauntingly apt manuscript for a moment, allowing himself a little time to gloat before handing it over to Cleo.

Putting aside her magazine, she frowned as she read the title. *"Bride of Darkness?"*

Michael tried to avoid a triumphant smile and failed. "It's a classic story, one that was never actually filmed, but it's been on the back burner at any number of production houses for years. Decades, if you want to know the truth."

Now Cleo examined the name of the scriptwriter. "Who is Bernie Williams?"

"A writer," Michael said evasively. "He's been around for a while."

A very long while—close to two hundred years. Bernie was a nightwalker who supported himself doing rewrites of medium-budget horror films, but he'd always wanted to do a script of his own. Unfortunately this particular one, a factual account of ancient nightwalker history, had never actually seen the light of film.

All the big studios had read and liked the script to the point of putting up money on it, but ultimately each had rejected it based on the notion that it was too far-fetched and wouldn't bear up under the scrutiny of a modern audience. The fact that it was all true, and some of those studio heads actually knew that, was beside the point.

Cleo turned to the page where the characters were listed and paled as she saw the particulars. "This is a vampire script, Michael."

"Sort of, it was written by someone who knows a lot about the subject. It is a factually based story."

"Factually based… You mean this was written by a nightwalker?" Cleo looked appalled. "Suppose someone actually believed it? It would be proof that the parafolk exist and we could all be destroyed!"

Michael raised his hand, placating her. "It is very hard to destroy us…and besides, those who understood the script knew about us anyway. It isn't that big a secret that parafolk are real. It's just not a public secret."

Ever the actress, Cleo rolled her eyes. "Not a public secret. Okay, I guess I can understand that. It means that some people know, but they don't make a big deal about knowing."

"There isn't a big deal to make. We aren't that different from anyone else, Cleo. Most of us are model citizens. Some even help out the authorities when they want to take advantage of our special skills. Outside of the Watchers, no one really believes we are evil, and those folks take exception to anyone different from themselves. If we weren't around they'd go after gays or some other minority."

Shaking her head, Cleo returned to studying the script. "So where did you want to start?"

"I thought we'd work on the conversion scene."

Her head went up immediately. "The what?"

"The scene where the heroine gets turned into a nightwalker." Michael consulted his copy of the script. "It begins on page forty-five. I'll take the part of the Count, while you are Emily."

She nodded slowly but was obviously not happy about it. "Do you want to do it in costume?"

He grinned at her. "It would film better. The scene begins with a love scene on a wedding night so just slip on one of the nightgowns. We'll use the bed in the corner." Still grinning, he headed for the small makeup table in the corner. "I'll be over here getting my fangs on straight."

In spite of her apparent reservations, Cleo laughed and Michael decided she was okay with his choice of script after all.

As he applied the fixative to the prosthetic fangs and slipped them into his mouth, Michael wondered at how his experiment with Cleo was going. He had to admit he was concerned. Tomorrow his time alone with her would be up and while he fully intended to keep his promise and release her, he still hoped to convince her to keep him on as her companion.

The last two nights had been wonderful. Under the spell of the camera Cleo had come alive, aglow under the film lights, her mood euphoric. Obviously she'd missed performing these past decades. In fact, she'd been starving for it, as much as she'd been starved for sex and for the fresh blood he offered.

Stroking his still blemish-free neck, he wished she'd left the marks of at least one of her feedings. Several times she'd bitten him there, but she was always careful to remove the marks. He still had the ones on his cock but those weren't the kind of marks a man wanted to show off. If he stayed her companion, he'd have to insist on her giving him proper marks. Neck or chest would be good. Even on his wrist.

Any place but under his cock.

He sighed, staring at his befanged reflection in the mirror. It was perfect between them. Why couldn't she see it and make it permanent? He couldn't imagine giving her up tomorrow even though he knew he'd have to if she insisted.

Now more than ever he knew how much he wanted her in his life. Even now she'd changed things for the better. He no longer drifted through the world, taking advantage of his gifts to make money without giving anything back, living with others rather than making a home of his own. In a few days he'd collect the key of the first place he'd bought on his own, and he was seriously looking into setting up Fly by Night Films.

None of that would have happened if it hadn't been for Cleo. He needed her. No, it was more than need. He was in love with her.

But he was certain she was in love with him and she probably hadn't loved anyone since her maker had died.

For a moment sudden anger overtook him. Rodriquez, the renegade. He'd seen a picture of the man once, looking every inch the Latin lover. The guy had probably been a real stud in bed.

How could an ordinary Irish-Scotch mix of a man like him compete with that? He didn't even look all that sexy. Not that Cleo had complained, but then again she hadn't been out all that much.

On a whim, he dipped his hand into the hair gel and used it to slick back his brown wavy hair, making himself look more like Cleo's maker. When he smiled the fangs winked at him and he startled then grinned. He actually did look a little like Rodriquez.

"I'm ready, Michael." Her beautiful voice came from behind him and he turned to see a vision in low-cut white lace, the loveliest of the costume nightgowns. With her dark hair unbound and flowing down to her shoulders, Cleo looked every inch the vampire's bride.

For an instant Michael imagined her as a real bride and he the bridegroom. If they were bloodmates, as he suspected they could be, then they might as well be married.

Well, yeah, but first he had to keep her marks — any of her marks — past tomorrow. Then they'd see about being bloodmates.

Cleo startled when she saw what he'd done to his appearance but recovered quickly. For a moment Michael wondered at her expression. It hadn't been desire in her lovely eyes but fear.

Even so, she said nothing and led the way to the bed, where the scene directed them to begin. In the script it was the Count's wedding night to the lovely Emily, and the night he turned her into one of his own kind.

The cameras were already set up to go, so Michael started them and followed her, his body already eagerly anticipating another heavy love scene. Their early evening lovemaking had only whetted his appetite and he wanted more. He just couldn't get enough of sex with Cleo.

Fortunately she seemed to feel the same way. Her eyes glowed faintly as she lay against the white linens of the pillows, the lace of her nightgown only slightly paler than her ultra-white skin, in stark contrast to her night-black hair.

His cock got so hard he thought he might explode.

"And now I have you all my own, my sweet Emily," Michael said deepening his voice and trying for something resembling a "Count"-type voice. Cleo's instant amusement told him that he hadn't managed it too well, but he didn't mind her laughing at him. He wasn't supposed to be the actor here.

Fortunately what he wanted to do with Cleo didn't actually require acting.

She held out her arms to him. "My dear Count. I await your pleasure."

"It is a pleasure just to behold your loveliness." Leaning in, he kissed her, their mouths and tongues meeting. As always he kept clear of her fangs, not wanting to prick his tongue. Cleo's tongue briefly entered his mouth, but as soon as she felt his new dentition it fled and she only kissed him with her lips.

Apparently French kissing a nightwalker hadn't been one of her favorite activities, he reasoned. That was odd because she certainly enjoyed kissing him that way.

He slid closer to her on the bed. "I enjoy your beauty, but I would see more of it." He pulled one of the thin straps holding up her gown off her shoulder, slipping it down so her breast was revealed. Immediately the nipple pebbled, ready for his taste and touch.

"I see your beauty," he said, "but would know the flavor of my beloved Emily."

Leaning over, he drew the nipple into his mouth, sucking it slowly. His fake fangs slid across them and he had to be careful not to break the skin. A little of Cleo's blood wouldn't convert him, but you could never be too careful. After all he wanted to be her companion, not join her as a nightwalker.

At least Cleo didn't mind his fangs on her breasts. She moaned under his careful suckling, her back arching beneath him. Each time he tugged on her nipple her mind sent out a tendril of golden desire, spooling around his. It was all Michael could do to not open up completely to her, but he wanted to avoid that for now. It would be easier to stick to the script if they weren't joined mentally.

He moved to the other breast, leaving his hand to play with the one he'd abandoned. Cleo's hips shifted on the bed and she cried out. "More, more…please."

It wasn't quite what the script had said, but Michael didn't think a little improvisation would hurt matters. He pulled her gown down past her waist and laid a line of kisses down the stretch of her belly, finally reaching the cleft between her legs.

How many times had he savored her sweetness here in the past few days? Eight? Ten? A dozen times? Many times, he knew, in addition to the time he'd made love to her as Lord Havamore but every time she'd tasted as fresh and new as the last. Cleo's pussy had a luscious flavor and he knew he could never get tired of it.

Never. Not in a hundred years.

For a brief moment Michael wished an odd thing. He suddenly wished that Cleo wasn't a nightwalker and that he didn't want to be her companion. For a bare moment in time he wanted her to be a normal human woman. He wished he could propose marriage to her, making truth out of the fiction of this being their bridal night.

But he knew he was thinking too much. Cleo couldn't be other than what she was, and truth was he loved her for it. He'd never wish her to be anyone else.

Michael took a long lick at her clit and Cleo arched off the bed, her hands finding his head. Again he felt her startle as she felt the oil in his hair, and she tried to surreptitiously wipe her hands off on the sheets.

More and more this confused him. He'd thought that by mimicking Rodriquez he could find a way past her defenses, but it didn't seem like she remembered her maker fondly at all. Nothing that reminded her of him pleased her.

Tearing himself away from her sweet pussy, Michael rose over her. "And now, sweet Emily, it is time for you to join with me. I will take your blood and feed you mine and then we will be lovers forever."

To his surprise, Cleo's expression froze then turned to one of horror.

"No" she whispered then repeated the word in a shout. She flung herself out from under him while Michael sat up in amazement.

Shaking, she crouched at the edge of the bed, her hands covering her face. "I can't do this, Michael, not even for you. It was bad enough the first time—I won't go through it again!"

Michael stared at her. "Won't go through what again? What are you talking about, Cleo?"

She hugged herself, more distressed than Michael had ever seen her. "Conversion. I won't do it, not even in pretend. I won't act this scene out. It was bad enough before. With him. You can't make me do it again." Her whole body seemed to shudder.

He didn't understand. "With Rodriquez? You mean when you were converted? But…"

Something occurred to Michael. Something awful…terrible…something completely against the laws he'd been taught to believe in. Something no nightwalker would ever do. But everyone knew that Rodriquez had been a renegade, an outlaw who was unwilling to follow the rules. And she'd said "make me do it again". It was just possible…

"Cleo…when you were converted…when you became a nightwalker…" He took a deep breath. "Was it your idea? I mean, you knew and agreed…"

She raised her head and stared at him, and Michael had never seen her as stunningly beautiful as she was just then.

Then she slowly shook her head and the heartbreak in her eyes nearly destroyed him.

"No, Michael, it wasn't my idea. He wanted someone like him around and so he picked me because he'd seen some of my films and was something of a fan. We went out to dinner, and I wondered why he didn't eat much, but he'd said he didn't care for the food and would get something later. I had no idea I was on the menu," she said with no little sarcasm.

"We went back to his house and it was large and impressive. He took me to his bed and then..." Her voice trailed off, it seemed to Michael that she stifled a sob.

"I had no inkling of what Rodriquez was up to. He took my blood then fed me his. The next thing I knew it felt like I was on fire, my body cramping, and when it finished my life as an actress, the world I lived in was lost to me. I never even realized it would be the last time I'd see the sun..." Her composure fled and for the first time Michael saw tears welling and overflowing her eyes. Even when she'd been upset before, she hadn't cried.

Cleo shook and one sob after another erupted from her. Without another thought Michael threw his arms around her and held her close as seventy years of pain, loneliness and frustration poured out of her. A long time to feel alone and betrayed by someone she'd trusted.

He held her as the storm of tears ran its course, murmuring words of comfort. Meaningless words in some sense but he hoped how he cared came through.

What she'd been through—converted against her will? Michael had no words for the fury he felt. For the first time in his life he felt as if he could do murder and if it had been possible he'd have gone back in time and been the one to stake the malevolent Rodriquez himself, preferably before he'd changed this woman's life.

When at last her tears stopped and she lay in his arms, quiet and apparently content to be there, he gave voice to what was in his heart.

"It's not supposed to be like that, Cleo. Conversion is a choice…it is always supposed to be a choice and I've never heard of any nightwalker violating that rule. You shouldn't have been changed without full knowledge of what you would become."

To his surprise, she gave a small, only slightly bitter laugh. "I know that now. I read the script. Bernie outlined it all and before this scene the Count tells Emily what he wishes of her and leaves it her choice to convert." She sighed.

"I know what should have happened…and what didn't. I guess Rodriquez didn't trust that I'd let him convert me and that's why he did it without my permission. Emily's count was willing to give her up if she wished."

"That's the way it is supposed to be, Cleo. No one should take another person's choices away. Even between you and me that was true. That's why I had to give you the choice of not keeping me as your companion, even if I did bend the rules to make you give me a fair tryout."

Her laugh was less bitter this time. "I don't think I mind anymore your ways of persuading me. It's funny. When I'm with you, I don't mind being a nightwalker. You make me feel special."

"You are special, Cleo. You always have been."

She looked up him and Michael thought he could read her entire soul in her eyes. "I don't think I want to act any more or be in front of a camera. I think…" She stopped. "I want to be real for the rest of the night."

He didn't blame her. "That's fine with me. I want things real between us."

Her face changed and Michael couldn't read her expression, but he knew something else bothered her. If only she'd open her mind completely then he'd understand and know how to address her concerns. Outside of when they had sex, she still kept her thoughts shuttered.

He'd have to use words to get the information he wanted. "What is it, Cleo?"

"I was thinking. Perhaps we need a change of scene."

A change? "Where would you like to go?"

"The beach house. Could we go there?"

Suddenly that sounded wonderful. He'd never even gotten a chance to show her the upstairs master bedroom that overlooked the ocean. He was planning something similar to it for the bedroom of his new home, only with luck he'd have a four-poster bed to fill it. "Sure, Cleo. Pack up the rest of your clothes and we can go tonight. There is still plenty of time until dawn."

Chapter Ten

ഔ

The beach house was just as she remembered it from her brief visit—full of movie posters, comfort and peace. They opened the windows to the ocean and the pounding sound of the surf and smell of the sea filled the room. It was all so welcoming and familiar. Funny how much she could remember about the place given how few hours she'd spent there.

It must have been a very special few hours to make such an impression.

Cleo could feel Michael's gaze on her as she moved about the downstairs living area. Unsure of what to say, she went into the kitchen and grabbed a bag of serum from the refrigerator. After pouring some of the contents into a glass she turned to him. "Do you want something?"

"I'll take a beer."

Cleo opened one and handed it to him then watched as he took a deep sip. She opened her mind just a little and sensed its tart, yeasty taste before he swallowed.

That had happened several times over the past few days and she wondered what it meant. It was like there was a back door he'd opened into his mind, and seemingly at will she was able to collect tastes and sensations that were his. In addition she also knew many of his thoughts, making it easy to anticipate his wants and needs.

For certain she knew Michael's feelings almost as soon as he did. He still couldn't read her, not quite the way she could him, but for her he was as transparent as air.

It was heady to be so close to someone—almost like being in their skin. She knew Michael. Knew his likes, dislikes and a lot of his history. At times he thought about other women he'd known, brief memories of dark hair, smooth skin and sweet kisses. He remembered sex with them but mostly when he thought of sex, he thought of her.

As she thought on it many of the women he'd cared about before had resembled her in one way or another. But he'd rarely had a long relationship with a woman. For some reason he'd never really loved before.

Well, that wasn't exactly true. It wasn't like he didn't love. It was just that he didn't love any of his former women. She took another look at the posters on the wall, the ones featuring her face and name. Michael hadn't just started to love her in the past few weeks. He'd loved her for a long time.

He'd loved her all along.

She'd only known him a short time, but she knew she loved him as well. They had a relationship—two people, in love with each other. In all of her long life she'd hadn't had anything as precious before. There was only one problem—she was immortal and Michael wasn't.

To her that was a problem.

Sure he hadn't aged much while Vlad's companion, but he'd still aged some. Even now she could see small lines at the corners of his face and could envision them growing deeper as the years went on. It would take a long time, but Michael would grow older. He'd age, grow infirm and eventually die.

When he died it would tear her heart out and she couldn't live with that. Even when Rodriquez had died she'd lost some of her self. She couldn't lose Michael.

Dying was the fate of all creatures unlike her—and unlike Michael if she could persuade him to join her. That was the solution she saw. She'd convert him as she'd been converted and then they'd live together forever.

Cleo had finally made up her mind about what she wanted and it wasn't a companion. If Michael wanted to be with her he'd have to convert. Like Rodriquez, she wanted someone like herself to love and that was what she'd brought Michael here for.

She would leave it his choice, but she didn't see a problem with that. He didn't mind her being a nightwalker. Surely he would enjoy it himself.

Michael moved to the open window and stared at the ocean. "The moon is full, Cleo. Come see." He beckoned to her and she joined him in gazing out onto the ocean, the moon's reflection a bright rippling streak on the dark water that stretched to the horizon.

"It's beautiful." She snuggled under his arm, sipping her serum while Michael drank his beer. His body was warm against hers, keeping away the chill of the salt-laden air. Humanly warm, a few degrees hotter than she was.

She could fly tonight but she didn't want to do it alone. She could carry him but wasn't sure if he'd enjoy that. Maybe tomorrow night they could both fly—after he was a nightwalker too.

Finally he put his empty bottle down. "Come upstairs, Cleo. There is something I've been wanting to show you."

His arm stretched around her waist, they took the stairs side-by-side until they reached a large open room with a wall of windows facing the sea. The view was spectacular, overlooking the beach and the moonlit ocean.

Heavy metal shades were folded against the wall near the window. Michael pointed to them. "They're on a light-sensitive switch. As soon as the sky stops being dark they cover the window. They also close in case of earthquake or power failure, just to be safe." He put his arms around her.

"Vlad had this room made especially for nightwalkers. You never need to fear the sun in here."

She sank onto the bed in the center of the room and noticed how she could still see the moon's path on the water. Michael turned off the overhead lamp and the only light came from outside.

Cleo felt like she was glowing, both from the moon and the man near her. She opened her arms. "Make love to me, Michael."

He smiled. "My pleasure, Lady Nightwalker."

Michael pulled off his shirt and unfastened his pants, releasing his erection to wave proudly at her. Moments later his clothes were on the floor and he was on the bed with her, caressing her and helping her out of hers.

He took his time undressing her, kissing her skin as it was revealed. He uncovered her breasts first—laying each one bare and sucking each nipple as if it were the first time he'd seen them. He whispered soft words to her, of how much he cared for her and how much she meant to him. Cleo took in every word, every compliment.

She loved him. With her body and her mind, she wanted him, with her, for all time. There was nothing ordinary between them. Sex had stopped being casual long ago.

Michael was her mate and tonight she'd see to it he'd be with her forever.

"What are you thinking?" Michael's voice interrupted her thoughts.

It was too soon to talk about now. Later, when they'd finished making love and he was sleepy and more receptive. That's when she'd ask him.

Cleo turned her most reassuring smile on him. "I'm thinking what a wonderful lover you are."

His sexy smile met hers. "We must be sharing our minds then, because I'm thinking the same thing about you."

She sat up and pushed him to lie back on the bed. Recumbent, he looked like a living statue in the moonlight streaming through the window.

A beautiful man — hers.

"It's been a while since I've tasted you, Michael. Will you let me go down on you now?" She licked her lips and saw Michael unconsciously repeat her action.

He leaned up on one elbow. "Do you promise to give me proper marks later if you remove the ones on my cock?"

"I promise," she said quickly. After all, he wouldn't need marks when she'd turned him.

Michael nodded slowly. "I think I can trust you now, Cleo." He leaned back against the pillows, quiet, only the rapid rise and fall of his chest indicating his excitement. Well, that and the gleam in his eyes. "I have to admit, I've missed your mouth on me."

Kneeling between his legs, Cleo reached for his cock and stroked it with her hand. Michael made a sharp hissing sound and in her mind, Cleo knew how exquisite he found her touch. She leaned forward to gently lick the tip of his cock.

"I've missed it too," she told him. Then her lips closed over him and she could no longer speak.

Michael had nothing intelligible to say, too overwhelmed by her mouth on him to make any sense at all.

It was the most thorough blowjob she'd ever given. Her questing tongue and lips missed no quarter-inch of his cock. Cleo ran one hand along his shaft while the other stroked the head and she gently licked his scrotum.

It was on the latter that she finally found the marks she'd left. On the underside of his balls she found two tiny scratches spaced as far apart as her fangs. Carefully she licked them until they were gone and was careful not to leave any more. After that she spent her time sucking on his tip, catching on her tongue the sweet fluid leaking from him.

Michael groaned aloud, fisting his hands in her hair, encouraging her to take him deeper in her mouth. Cleo obliged, still careful not to leave any marks from her fangs.

Finally Michael pulled her up to lie on top of him. His brown eyes turned gold in the light of the moon. "Enough foreplay for me, your turn." He rolled her over and licked his way down her torso until he reached the apex of her legs. "Open for me Cleo. Show me your secrets."

She had secrets…but they weren't between her legs. Not that it mattered when Michael leaned forward to blow a gentle puff of hot air across her clit. Cleo settled back against the pillows and watched Michael's mouth disappear between her thighs before she felt it close on her nether lips, his tongue reaching deep into her folds. He plied his lips and teeth to her, sucked and blew alternately until she could barely remember her own name, much less what she wanted from him.

What she wanted from him—love everlasting. Yes, that was it. She wanted Michael's everlasting love.

But for now she'd make do with his mouth on her pussy, making her feel like the most beloved woman alive.

Michael was one man who really knew how to make a woman feel good down there. His tongue seemed prehensile as it poked, prodded and slipped around her clit and folds, and when it slid inside her Cleo couldn't have stopped her release even if she'd wanted to. And she didn't want to.

"That's so good, Michael…yes…like that." Her words became disjointed, her mouth as disconnected from her brain as the rest of her seemed to be. A brief cry followed as her first orgasm since midnight swept over her.

Michael really knew how to show a lady nightwalker a good time. But enough was enough. Using her strength, Cleo pulled Michael up and held his shoulders so he was suspended above her. His cock rested just at the apex of her legs. She could feel the head pressing at her center but he made no move to enter. It was up to her.

For a long moment they gazed into each other's eyes.

Finally Cleo managed to reconnect her mouth to her brain. "Enough foreplay, Michael. Let's fuck."

His slow grin told her he appreciated her brief descent into vulgarity. "Whatever you say." His hips surged forward, his cock finding her pussy and invaded it, filling her completely. The end of his cock hit the opening to her womb and then they were connected.

It was the first time she'd felt his complete strength during lovemaking. Cleo clutched at his shoulders at the power of that stroke. She knew now he'd always held back a little. Perhaps worried she'd be hurt by him, but he couldn't hurt her.

Michael had told her that companions were stronger than normal humans and she now understood just how much stronger they were. That stroke might have broken the pelvis of a normal human woman.

Fortunately she was anything but normal and his power turned her on like nothing she'd ever felt before. "Oh, Michael," she whispered. It was an inadequate response but the only one she had.

Michael's face showed a similar astonishment to what she felt. He caught her hands and pulled them off his shoulders. He pulled them high over her head, and with his cock deep inside and his hips holding down hers, it effectively immobilized her. Cleo knew she could break free if she wanted to…maybe. Or maybe not.

But it didn't matter because truthfully she didn't want to. She wanted Michael's strength and power. She wanted him to dominate her tonight.

His voice was harsher than normal, studded with need and desire. "Hang on, I'm going to show you something you haven't ever seen before."

Cleo couldn't help her shudder at his declaration, but even mostly helpless in his grasp she couldn't resist his challenge.

"Do your worst, baron...I'm not afraid of you." It was a line from a costume drama called *Bride of the Outlander*, one of her least recognized movies but one that was a secret favorite as it had been one of the few she'd done with a real love scene.

She hadn't expected Michael to recognize it, but he did. He grinned at her and gave her the hero's answering line. "It is not my worst you need be afraid of, my lady, but my best." He leaned forward and grinned into her face, improvising the next line. "And my best happens now."

Michael surged inside her again and scripts, lines, movies and all else fled Cleo's mind. All that was left of her consciousness was the two of them on a bed in the moonlight with his cock pumping in and out of her and driving her wild.

She gave in to Michael's driving strokes, clutching his back as he reared above her. Her head ran into the pillow behind her and soon she was pleased it was there as the headboard would have been a harder thing to be hitting. She reached back and clutched the pillow around her head, holding onto it as if it were a life preserver in a sea of sensation.

His strokes started a fire within her, flames hot enough to burn away all of her inhibitions. In addition a hunger grew, bloodlust rising from the smell of his skin in her nostrils. She lifted her head to lick his chest and tasted his salty sweetness. She found a vein and bit deep, letting his blood fill her mouth. Michael bucked when her teeth sank into him, but even through the purple-blue sensual haze of his mind she felt his approval of her action.

What my lady needs, she may have.

So good. She drank deep of him as he filled her over and over.

Michael's mind broke through haze of bloodlust. *Stop now, Cleo.*

She didn't want to stop but she obeyed him, ending her drink and erasing the wounds from his chest. Passion in her rose and overwhelmed and she cried out when she felt Michael clench at the very edge of orgasm. She looked to see his eyes staring wild and intense. *Join with me, Cleo. Feel my love for you.*

Words never spoken aloud between them. She opened her mind and they joined, their thoughts stumbling over each other and jumbling together during the height of passion. She felt the triumph in Michael's mind right before he moved one last time and released deep within her, the heat of his cum flooding her and rocketing her again into climax.

Both of them cried aloud simultaneously as their bodies and minds came together.

Their minds open, her thoughts and his commingled and slid over each other as they rested, the physical afterglow of their bodies matching the deep satisfaction in their minds.

She'd never opened her mind like that to anyone, not even her maker. Not willingly before. But this wasn't anything like that had been. This was Michael, her lover and her friend.

Companion. He spoke directly into her mind along the link. *Companion…and maybe bloodmate. We will see.*

Bloodmate? She wasn't so sure of that. But it didn't matter because she wanted him to be like her.

Like you?

Too late Cleo remembered that their minds were joined with nothing to keep her thoughts away from him.

Michael sat up and leaned over her, his dark hair lying heavy on his brow. His eyes were deadly serious, no hint of amusement in them. *What are you thinking, Cleo? I have no wish to become a nightwalker. I'm happy the way things are.*

I thought...but... You like nightwalkers. Like being around them. I thought you'd want to be one.

He shook his head. *You thought wrong.*

Cleo couldn't miss how emphatic that thought was. Even so, she continued to argue her point. *But Michael — you will grow old. You'll die.*

All living things do, my lady. Even nightwalkers can die. There is no shame in that. The shame is in not living the life you are given.

She pulled away from him, mentally as well as physically. Michael's eyes showed pain as she closed the link between them but that didn't stop her. Feeling more than naked before him, she wrapped the sheet around her and spoke aloud. "You are saying you would refuse the vampire's gift?"

"I am saying I enjoy who I am, Cleo. Eternity isn't a gift I want."

"Even with me?" The words were hard to say, but she didn't want to open her mind to him now, not when there was so much wrong between them. Still she had to tell him. "I love you, Michael. I couldn't stand by while you age and die."

Mixed emotions showed on his face — delight over her declaration, pain from her distress. He put his arms out and captured her in them.

"I love you too, Cleo. I want to be with you for as long as that is possible. As your companion that can be a very long time, more than several normal human lifetimes."

He took a deep breath and his expression grew somber. "You have to remember what you are asking when you ask me to convert. Remember what it was like for you. I enjoy the feel of the sun on my face and the daylight hours you can't see. I enjoy eating what I want. When we are linked I can share all that with you.

"That's part of being a companion, even more than feeding you and healing your ills. That's what I've tried to show you for the past few days, just how great it can be to have a companion so you'd let me be yours."

He shook his head. "I admire nightwalkers, but I don't want to be one. I want to be your companion, and maybe your bloodmate, but nothing more."

Tears welled in her eyes, the second time she'd felt them in longer than she could remember. Earlier she'd cried when she'd told Michael how Rodriquez had converted her — now she cried because Michael wouldn't let her convert him. For so long she'd cared so little about anything, good or ill, tears hadn't been necessary.

Michael made her remember how sad the world could be.

Had she even cried when Rodriquez had died? But then all she'd lost was a master. Michael meant far more than that to her. He was her anchor in the world, someone to hold and love. But not forever. Not forever because as much as he loved her, he also wanted the sun on his face.

She cried and he held her, murmuring softly into her ear, comforting words that meant nothing. When she ran out of tears, he still held her close.

He held her chin, his eyes dark in the moonlight. "I'm sorry I've upset you. That wasn't my intention." A laugh escaped him. "It's sweet of you to want me around for so long. Not that you could have done it. It takes a lot of blood loss to turn a companion—they are almost impossible to turn."

But you aren't a companion, she wanted to say, but she didn't. He wouldn't know yet that she'd removed the marks and he would soon revert to a normal human... Well normal except for having superb psychic powers.

Soon he'd be a regular human again and this time he wouldn't have the excuse of being her companion as a reason to hunt for her when she left. Which she was going to do as soon as possible. The three days were now over and she'd made up her mind.

They weren't linked but she could still feel that back door into his mind open to her. She sent into it a suggestion of extreme weariness. Michael blinked then yawned as her command took effect.

He tried a weak smile. "Come, Cleo. I can feel how tired you are. It's going to grow light soon. We can discuss everything more at rising." He lay on the bed and held out his arms. Cleo allowed him to pull her close, still sending waves of weariness to him.

With his mind so susceptible to hers, it only took a minute before he was sound asleep and she could slip out of his arms.

The sun would be rising in less than an hour but it wouldn't take her that long to get where she was going. With a full moon outside she could fly to her Santa Monica home faster than a car would take her. While Michael slept, Cleo dressed quickly and quietly.

Before leaving she took one last look at him still spread out on the bed. He'd be her love forever, but she couldn't stay with him, not this way. Slipping out of the bedroom, Cleo ran down the stairs to the living room and out onto the porch that opened onto the beach. She left her bag behind — there was only one pair of underwear in it anyway and she had more in her house. Of course she'd have to sleep on the floor tonight since her bed was still at the studio, but she'd done worse.

She'd make Michael return it and the rest of her belongings tomorrow evening. Leaving him now would reinforce her position and he'd have to accept her rejection or she'd take it to his vaunted Parafolk Council.

Cleo climbed onto the railing and balanced there for a moment, staring at the sand far below. The moon was low on the horizon and she could feel the impending dawn but she could still fly to where she was going.

Lifting her arms, Cleo rose into the air to hover above the railing. As it always did, flying under the moonlight made her smile, a brief euphoria that drew away some of her pain at leaving Michael behind. Moving slowly out over the beach, she turned and headed toward the lights of town to the south.

Caught in the spell of flight she didn't hear the dart or see the man who'd fired it. All she felt was a sharp pain in her upper back and then a great weariness slipped through her. Next thing she fell from the sky until the sand stopped her fall and she lay collapsed on it, her limbs oddly frozen. Cold and gritty under her cheek, the sand smelled of the ocean, but then another odor came to her, that of a normal man.

Make that men, she thought as three men ran to her across the sand. In moments Cleo was surrounded, covered with a blanket and bundled off to a waiting car. Unceremoniously, she was thrown onto the backseat where one of her captors already sat. He pulled her to the corner and fastened a seat belt around her paralyzed body.

"We saw her fly," said one of the men in the front seat, his voice laced with excitement. "She must be one of them."

The man next to her pulled on the blanket, unwrapping it from around her head. He pulled up her upper lip and touched her fangs. His finger tasted terrible and she wrinkled her nose in disgust.

"Yeah, she's a vampire all right." He sounded jubilant. "Staking this place out was a good idea after all."

Somehow she found her voice through the creeping paralysis. "What do you want?"

The man sitting with her ignored her question. "Okay, get this car moving. We need to get her inside before the sun rises." He laughed, the sound of it evil as he threw the blanket over her face again. Whatever had been in the dart continued to work on her body, but Cleo fought unconsciousness for as long as she could. She had to know what these men wanted.

Unfortunately, the last thing she heard was from the man in the front seat. "Yeah, we need to keep her out of the sun. We wouldn't want her to burst into flames too soon."

Chapter Eleven

ഌ

Phinious Jones, the Supreme High Watcher of the Paranormal Watchers Society, was a short, pudgy man with bad skin, thin white hair and a nasty body odor. Very nasty — Cleo gagged when he sat next to her that evening. She would have preferred another seating arrangement, but the drug they'd given her made her limbs reluctant to obey and she couldn't move away when he decided to sit on her bed, that being the only place to sit.

He breathed out, and she noticed his breath was even worse. This time she had to work on controlling her nausea. It wouldn't do to throw up on him, particularly when the only thing in her stomach was Michael's blood.

Between her, Phinious and the three bodyguards who'd been designated her personal "watchers", the room was overcrowded. It wasn't much bigger than a closet with a bathroom anyway, but at least it didn't have any windows to board up against the sun.

It didn't have any windows for her to escape through either, or to let in the fresh night air, which would have been welcome given the odiferous nature of her visitor.

The High Watcher seemed almost grandfatherly as he patted her hand. "Now my dear, you know what we want. First of all, we know that Deloris DeNight isn't really your name. There is no birth record corresponding to it."

Cleo shrugged. "A lot of people have stage names. That isn't against the law." She crossed her arms and glared at her "host". "On the other hand drugging, kidnapping and holding someone against their will is."

He ignored her last comment. "You are a vampire, Ms. DeNight. You were caught flying under a full moon."

She laughed. "Don't be ridiculous! There are no such things as vampires. I wasn't flying. I jumped off the balcony to the sand and your people shot me with a dart."

"That's not what they said they saw."

She narrowed her eyes at him. "Then they were mistaken."

"You don't go into the sun."

"I'm extremely sensitive to it. Lots of people are. It makes me break out in big red splotches. Having an allergy isn't a crime nor does it mean that I'm some sort of imaginary supernatural being."

"And you sleep all day."

"I'm up all night. That's when I do my TV show, so of course I sleep during the day. If you kidnapped everyone in Hollywood that did that, you'd have to snag half the town." She looked around. "This room would get awfully crowded. Not that it isn't already."

"You have fangs..."

"False ones! I explained that before. I used the wrong glue on my prosthetics a while ago and haven't been able to knock them free. The dentist said they would loosen eventually." She tried a lighthearted laugh. "My boyfriend said he thought they were cute."

The grandfatherly persona turned sad. "Your boyfriend...you mean Mr. Brown, whose home you were at. We've known about his proclivities for a long time. He's high on our watch list as a known vampire sympathizer."

Cleo rolled her eyes. "Mr. Brown and I have been dating for a while. I've never seen him with a vampire."

"Other than yourself." Phinious smiled and for the first time Cleo felt real fear. His teeth were bright white and even, a perfect Hollywood smile. They were clearly his best feature, but the sight was more than unnerving. It was the evilest smile she'd ever seen.

She drew back and Phinious turned solicitous. "Your loyalty is commendable but I'm afraid it is misplaced. You say Mr. Brown is your boyfriend. You say he thinks your fangs are cute. And yet, in spite of his devotion, your boyfriend has not been pounding on our door to help you."

"He doesn't know where I am," Cleo countered.

"He does," Phinious said gleefully. "We sent him a note telling him that you were our guest and yet there has been no word from him or any of the others on our watch list. Not even the police have taken an interest in your whereabouts, and don't you think your boyfriend would have notified them? Don't you find that interesting?"

Cleo's fear intensified. Michael knew where she was and hadn't done anything about it? Could her leaving him really have angered him that much?

The benevolent grandfather was back. "I'm afraid you've been abandoned, young woman."

Young woman? In spite of everything, Cleo felt like snickering. She was half-again as old as Phinious.

"There is no reason to fear us. If you tell us what we want we won't hurt you."

"What do you want?"

The evil smile returned, this time with a hint of triumph in Phinious' beady eyes. "We want to know whatever you do about the others like you. Vampires, werewolves and other paranormal creatures. Who they are, what they do. Names and addresses. That sort of thing. And a confession, of course."

"A confession?"

"A signed confession that you are a vampire. What your real name is and when you were born, when you died and became what you are."

"I'm not dead," she said indignantly. "Nor do I sleep in a coffin. You are making a mistake. There are no such things as vampires, or werewolves, or those supernatural beings you mentioned."

There was a tap at the door and one of the watchers went to open it. A very excited man was on the other side brandishing a folder containing a sheaf of loose papers. "We found her, High Watcher. We know who she is!"

With a sinking sensation Cleo watched as Phinious opened the folder to reveal several old studio headshots of her, a list of her acting credits and a printout of a website page about her, plus a copy of her original birth certificate, dated 1906.

Phinious read through the material, grinning with obvious delight. "Cleopatra Lutz? The old movie actress?" He held up one of the pictures and looked at it and her. "That's where I'd seen you before — on the late-late show."

This wasn't the first time Cleo had had to explain the resemblance. "Of course I look like her. Cleopatra was my great-grandmother. I was even named after her, but I use Deloris DeNight professionally."

"Oh, and then where is your great-grandmother?"

"She's been dead nearly twenty years. Some small town in Montana I think, but I could be wrong," Cleo improvised. "She met my great-grandfather about seventy years ago and settled on a ranch out there. They had a son, who had a daughter, then I came along. My great-grandmother didn't approve of my grandmother, so they fell out of touch..." Cleo grew a family tree and its problems out of thin air while Phinious simply smiled his wicked smile and nodded.

Finally she ran out of material and he stopped nodding. "You know what I think? I think you're a very talented actress, Ms. Lutz. I also believe you are the original Cleopatra Lutz who never met a man from Montana or lived on a ranch with her son but became a vampire and has lived in the dark shadows of Los Angeles ever since."

He leaned over her and this time she recoiled away from him. "Are you going to give us that confession and the names of your co-monsters?"

Cleo summoned her courage and raised her chin. "I am not a monster and will sign nothing to that effect."

Phinious almost seemed pleased by her answer. "Very well. You are still within our control and we are going to use you to prove to the world that vampires exist—one way or another!"

* * * * *

"Cleopatra Lutz—Live at the Hollywood Bowl!" read the flyer.

For at least a few minutes, Cleo thought sadly, examining the paper that her watcher for the day had handed her. It advertised a special sunrise meeting of the Paranormal Watchers Society of the greater Los Angeles area, with her immolation by exposure to sunlight the main event.

What a terrible irony. Her biggest public appearance ever—at the Hollywood Bowl no less, a venue she'd always wanted to play—and it was going to be her last appearance at all. The PWS had made plans for a giant rally, offering proof to their membership and the press at large of the existence of parafolk. With her capture they had all the evidence they thought they needed.

She was a celebrity from long ago who was still alive, had fangs and would die when what appeared to be harmless sunlight hit her. It was perfect as far as they were concerned. All they had to do was tie her to a stake and wait until dawn. Her death would prove everything.

She tossed the flyer onto the table. "It isn't going to work the way you want it to. I'm not going to explode or burst into flames."

Of course her death wouldn't be nearly as spectacular as they were hoping. Between making their own films she and Michael had watched some modern vampire movies where the creatures had caught fire or evaporated into dust when staked or caught outside after sunrise. After laughing over the absurdity, Michael had taken the opportunity to explain to her what would really happen.

Nightwalkers didn't actually burn in sunlight. They suffered from massive UV poisoning and turned black as a result—so they looked like they'd been torched but it wasn't nearly as impressive as what was in the movies.

Fortunately her tendency to fall asleep as soon as the sun rose would make the experience reasonably painless for her, but it was still pretty humiliating to think that the last sight anyone would have of her would be her looking like she'd gotten caught in a flamethrower. Embarrassing to say the least.

For a moment she almost wished she would burst into flames. At least she could have gone out with a bang, in a fashion befitting her status as a former movie star. Instead her death would hardly merit a second-page mention in the trades. Not unlike the ignoble end to her career as a movie star, fading into the shadows after her conversion.

She doubted the crowd would even applaud.

Her slack-jawed jailor stared at her. "What do you mean you won't burn? You mean because you aren't a real vampire? Naw, I've seen your fangs, you're real all right."

She meant to correct him, at least to make him call her a nightwalker, but why bother. He probably wasn't bright enough to understand the need for political correctness anyway. Besides, she was still trying to convince them they'd made a terrible mistake.

Instead of arguing with him, she sat on the narrow bed and stewed over the situation as he closed and bolted the door from the outside.

Three days ago she'd been snatched from the sky by way of a poisoned dart and awakened that evening imprisoned in this lightproof room. She'd been watched by a constant guard of men with a natural resistance to mental pressure, kept in place by the locked door and the silver chain holding her ankle to the bed's frame.

Cleo took a moment to pull ineffectually on that last insult, taking care to wrap the edge of the sheet around her hand before tugging on it to avoid it burning her. It didn't budge—the links were still as solid as they had been originally. Nightwalkers had great strength, but she couldn't break a pure silver chain or its manacle.

She couldn't even stand it next to her skin. She'd wrapped a strip of towel around her ankle to protect it from the silver, telling her captors that she had a severe allergy to the metal.

They hadn't believed her. It didn't help that she also suffered from a severe allergy to the sun, a severe allergy to most foods and drink, had unusually pointed incisors and fell asleep at the break of dawn every day. Under the circumstances her captors were pretty convinced they had themselves a real vampire in custody.

Damn it.

The only thing they hadn't done was to provide her with anyone to drink from, instead sending in a fresh bag of blood every day. Of course she'd dutifully turned up her nose at it, still trying to convince them she really wasn't what they thought she was. She'd sworn to herself she wouldn't drink their canned blood no matter how hungry she got.

Her stomach growled, and once more Cleo wished that at least one of her guards could be mesmerized. Without linking to them, she couldn't get their cooperation to feed and after three days it was getting harder to ignore the bag of blood sitting on the bedside table.

They'd even given her a glass to pour it into. She picked it up and grimaced at the shatterproof plastic. How thoughtful, she wouldn't have to drink it from the bag. Of course she would have to chew a hole through the plastic first. They hadn't left her with a knife or pair of scissors. Apparently they were worried she'd try and take her own life.

Again, they were right. She might have.

No. Whatever else she did, she would not give them the satisfaction of knowing for sure what she was. Cleo took the glass to the sink in the nearby bathroom and filled it there, drinking heartily. Maybe if she drank enough water it would soothe the cramps in her stomach.

The door's opening took her by surprise, but not half as much as the man who slipped inside, looking furtively over his shoulder. He wasn't one of her usual jailors, she could tell as soon as he'd entered. They'd all been picked because of their resistance to mental control while her visitor's mind was an open book to her. Cleo couldn't help her gasp as she read what lay on those pages.

His name was Horace Brock and he believed she was a vampire...no surprise there. But he didn't want to see her dead. He wanted her to feed from him and make him like her.

Horace wanted to become a vampire too.

Cleo couldn't help but see the irony in it and she almost laughed. She'd been captured in part because Michael had refused the vampire's kiss, making her leave him and become vulnerable. This man wanted what her lover had refused and wanted it bad enough to break in here past her guards. He couldn't get her out, but that didn't matter to him.

It mattered to her though and besides she couldn't give him what he wanted. Making Horace into a vampire was totally against her principles and doing it would most likely give the Watchers more proof.

Besides, she'd never done a conversion before and didn't want him to be her first. On the other hand, she could use him for a quick snack.

She gave him a welcome smile and a push on his mind that left his eyes glazed and jaw hanging open. "Am I glad to see you," she murmured, just before nipping into his neck.

The taste of his blood was pleasant, if weak. She took several quick sips, but inwardly Cleo sighed. Drinking from Horace was too much like taking advantage of a pizza deliveryman, particularly when compared to the nectar she'd been drinking from Michael's veins.

Would she ever taste Michael's richness again? Most likely not since she'd run out on him twice now. He'd never forgive her, particularly since she'd removed the marks without replacing them and then run out on him. She'd waited until the full moon as they'd agreed, so she had fulfilled their bargain, but somehow she didn't think he'd really see things that way.

Without the marks he was no longer her companion and she had no rights to his blood…or his lovemaking. No rights at all. And yet she craved him.

Suddenly, taking Horace's blood seemed distasteful. It was an act of desperation, not that of a proper nightwalker. She closed and erased the marks of her fangs and let him go.

Her mind easily forced forgetfulness into his, as well as a strong desire to never go near her again. For a moment he stared at her as if wondering who she was then he stumbled from the room. Quickly, Cleo tried the door but it was locked again.

For a moment she wondered about that. If the door had been locked how had Horace gotten through, both in and out of her room? Cleo puzzled that for a moment before giving up.

She sank again onto the bed. Her thirst was quenched, but not her real hunger. Horace Brock had been strictly nutrition, nothing more, and drinking from him made her realize how much she'd come to rely on Michael. Now she knew just what she'd given up.

Why had she left him—because he didn't want to become like her, and he would force her to accept his mortality? But now she would die before him. It was ironic, this twist of fate. If she'd stayed with him she'd be safe and they would have had decades to be together. Instead she'd die soon.

Michael had been right. Anyone could die—it was how you lived that made the difference.

There was more too. For years she'd barely lived at all, surviving on the outskirts of all society, not even seeking out her own kind. Sure Rodriquez had told her she and he were the only vampires around, but at some level she'd known he'd been lying to her.

But she hadn't tried to find any others, even after her maker had died. Instead she'd given up her art and denied her talent to keep her obscurity. Long, wasted years of doing nothing, accomplishing nothing, being nothing to no one.

How could she have thought of this as "eternal life"? It was far closer to an eternal death. Michael's harebrained plan to open a studio for parafolk suddenly seemed a lot less harebrained. She could even see how they could get it started. There were plenty of people in the movie industry who'd jump at the chance to use real "special effect" artists in their works, people who could actually shapeshift or use magic to fly or cast spells to disappear. Their studio could hire out parafolk to the other studios to get the seed money to start their own productions…

Maybe they could even make that movie, *Bride of Darkness*.

Cleo's heart sank. Of course, that was presuming she could get out of her current predicament. The poster for her upcoming final starring appearance caught her eye. They were being distributed all over town, at least among the Watchers' set. Would Michael even see it? Would he care if he did? So far he hadn't done anything to help her even though Phinious had told her he and the others on their "watch list" knew where she was.

Would he know that she'd died thinking of him?

Even if some miracle happened and she found a way out of this mess, could she ever hope to gain his forgiveness? Would he ever take her to bed again, holding her and making her feel like a real woman?

So many questions. Cleo lay on the bed and wondered how she would ever find answers for them. It was possible she wouldn't. Maybe after ninety-nine years of life it was finally her time to die.

If only she could see him or get a message to him. She wanted so much to tell him how she felt. Anything so that he'd know how much she regretted having left him.

Two more days until the Paranormal Watchers' big event. Funny how having all the time in the world could turn into so little time left.

* * * * *

"You're sure she couldn't read you at all," Michael said.

"Only what I wanted her to see." Horace grinned at him. "She was too hungry to look deeper, so it was easy."

The spellcaster took a seat in Michael's PRUcom office — the company whose secret name was Parafolk R Us. For the past fourteen years Michael had held a position on the board of directors, it being one of his many ventures intended to make the world secure for other parafolk.

PRUcom's primary functions included acting as a holding company for private property owned by people whose unusually long life spans sometimes triggered embarrassing questions. Sometimes government officials got curious when a man paid taxes for more than a hundred years using the same name, but they never questioned when a company did the same thing.

Recently PRUcom had completed the purchase of the nearly abandoned Eagen Brothers lot, an action that for some reason hadn't reached the attention of any of the trade magazines, even if some reporters had heard rumors of a new studio being formed. No one messed with the parafolk or provided them unwelcome attention in Los Angeles. It just wasn't a wise thing to do.

Unfortunately those in the PWS weren't at all wise, which is why they were in this fix.

Michael ran his hand over his unshaved face and sat opposite the man who'd most recently seen Cleo. He knew he must look a mess, but he'd barely been outside the building in the past two days. Since her capture, his office had become the center of operations for him and he even slept on the couch, not wanting to leave in case there was news. Besides, a bed without Cleo would have felt far too lonely.

It would probably be wise to catch a shower and change clothes though, he thought wryly. Maybe later today.

"How did you convince her to feed from you?"

The spare man laughed. "I made it seem like I wanted her to turn me. That way she would have an excuse to take my blood."

"Oh?" Michael tried to keep his voice calm, but it was hard. He hadn't expected the powerful spellcaster to take that route while finding a way into Cleo's prison. Their spies inside the Watchers' headquarters had mentioned Cleo was refusing the blood bags, most likely trying to look as human as possible. That's when they'd hatched this scheme to sneak food into her. Or a food source anyway.

Horace was best suited for infiltrating their sworn enemies' camp. He was able to cloud even the strongest minds and he didn't mind getting nibbled on, making him the ideal choice to keep Cleo's strength up. Michael was too well known to do it himself. Still, he didn't like the idea of another man feeding his woman, much less offering to let himself be turned. It was too intimate, too much like what he'd turned down from her.

She'd offered to turn him and he'd refused, not wanting to lose his remaining humanity. Now he had nothing but humanity since she'd removed the marks. He wasn't even her companion anymore.

Cleo might be lost to him...but he didn't have to like it, and he certainly wasn't going to share her with another man.

"Take it easy, Michael." Ever perceptive, even without reading his thoughts, the spellcaster took hold of Michael's arm. "I didn't mean it, and she didn't want me, so you can relax. All I did was provide a quick snack. She hardly even fed from me and all I could sense were thoughts of you when she did it."

"Thoughts of me? Are you sure?" For the first time in sixty years, Michael felt like he was back in junior high school, asking if a girl liked him. "Did she say something?"

Laughing, Horace clapped him on the back. "No, she didn't, but she was thinking really hard. Like I said, she took less than a pint from me and I could feel how hungry she was."

He shook his head. "I wouldn't be surprised if she has trouble taking food from others in the future. She's kind of hung up on you so no one else tastes good. She even tried to tell me not to come back again. She'd rather starve than feed from me."

Keeping his face impassive, Michael felt an inward surge of satisfaction. Perhaps he could still win Cleo when this was over and she was rescued. Of course rescuing her had to be top priority. No point in worrying about his relationship with a woman if she was going to be dead in a couple of days. Not that that he was going to let that happen. He'd die before he let anyone hurt his Lady Nightwalker.

No, not just that. Cleo was more than just his nightwalker... Michael had never felt like this about Vlad. She was his lady more than anything else.

Michael tightened his hands into fists then unclenched them just as slowly and took a deep breath. "Thank you, Horace. I appreciate your help."

The slender man nodded and rose to leave. "Don't mention it, Michael. It was the least I could do. Besides, it's nice to meet a new nightwalker, especially one that's been lost all this time." He leaned back to admire the framed movie poster on the wall, one of Cleo's of course. "She really was great, wasn't she?"

"She still is," Michael said to himself as Horace left. He considered the videotapes in his bottom drawer, the results of their "screen tests". In between strategy sessions he'd spent the previous days reviewing them and two things were clear—first of all, Cleo still had great charisma in front of the camera, and second, he was going to have to seriously edit out the sex scenes they'd recorded before someone else saw them and got the bright idea of doing parafolk porn.

His cock got hard from remembering the images of Cleo and him locked together in loving embrace. The camera had even caught the occasional glimpse of her fangs buried in his neck or chest, the passion on her face as she'd drank from him.

Michael took a moment to shake his head ruefully. In his mind he knew why she'd left him and that there was no reason to believe she'd ever willingly come back. In fact, after she'd run out on him the second time, his head wondered how he could ever trust her to stay with him.

But his heart knew something different. He'd seen that look on her face when they'd made love and deep inside he believed that was the true measure of what she felt for him. Cleo loved him—pure and simple.

And he loved her and that was all that mattered. He'd get her back and they'd work out their differences, one way or another. It was a promise he made, both to her and to himself. They needed each other, and for more than sex or blood or longevity. Nothing mattered if he couldn't keep her safe from harm, particularly the kind of harm the PWS had planned.

Again fury slipped through him at how they'd staked out his home and waited for their return, then used a drugged dart on Cleo when she'd left the safety of his embrace. Even though she'd removed the marks he was still sensitive to her. He'd woken when she'd been hurt and had run to the balcony to see the men drag her away. Too late to rescue her, he'd found the dart on the sand where she'd fallen and had it analyzed.

It held an interesting potion, able to knock out a nightwalker. The city chief, Jonathan, had been very concerned about the dart and the PWS and had authorized Michael and his team to do whatever was necessary to get Cleo back.

Not that Michael needed the chief's permission to go after their enemies. They'd drugged Cleo and dragged her away and now they planned to kill her in a public and painful fashion. For too long the parafolk, including him, had ignored the Watchers' actions, but they'd gone too far this time. Yes, the PWS were definitely unwise to mess with the parafolk.

He'd get Cleo back and in the process he and the others would teach the Watchers a lesson they would never forget!

Chapter Twelve

ഔ

It was a beautiful morning for an execution. The air above was free of clouds except for a few wispy streaks near the horizon, and the deep velvet sky was studded with stars. Not a lot of stars, of course, given the ambient glow of the city even at four a.m., but the pinpricks of light still delighted Cleo as she breathed in the cold crisp air of early morning. Even the itching from the silver chains around her wrists, waist and ankles didn't diminish her enjoyment of finally being outside.

She'd been locked up too long, five days solid, away from the night sky and open air and now she realized how much she'd missed it. A fine time to learn that she loved the night, two hours before her first — and last — dawn.

Phinious had visited her cell late the night before and had delighted in telling her just how the ceremony was to happen. They planned to use the dark pre-dawn time to show clips of some of her old movies, demonstrating just how old she was, then reveal her on stage tied to a stake, dressed in the same outfit from her last film and looking as young as she had been in the early thirties. Obviously she would have to be something other than a normal human being for that to be real.

Close-up cameras would reveal her fangs and stay on her face as the sun came up and the first rays hit her. They were hoping for something spectacular when that happened, in spite of how many times she'd told them that she wouldn't burst into flames.

Norms could be really stupid sometimes.

Cleo knew she should have been frightened, but as the limo pulled up to take her and her two guards across town to the outside theatre she couldn't help a tinge of actual excitement. The outfit they'd found, a white chiffon gown that clung to all the right curves, made her feel like a movie star again on her way to a big film debut. If she tried, she could even think of the cuffs and chains as some form of kinky jewelry.

Maybe if they had been made of white gold instead of pure silver...or platinum, since she didn't have a problem wearing either of those metals. This wasn't all that bad a look for her. Normally she didn't like looking into mirrors—Michael had assured her that no nightwalker did as they got older but didn't age—but with no one around to do her makeup she'd had to do it herself. She'd spent a long time gazing at her reflection and she'd been pleased with what she'd seen. Once more she looked like the movie star she'd been so long ago.

Michael would have been pleased too. Really pleased. In fact, she'd probably be able to get him hard just by breathing deeply, given how low the neckline of her gown was.

For not the first time she wondered if she'd see him again. Even after all this time she hoped for some kind of intervention from the parafolk, but there wasn't any sign of one. When she'd first stepped outside of the Watchers' hangout she'd looked but there had been no sign of Michael or any other kind of rescue team. Now, as they made their way through the streets of Los Angeles, she knew it was probably too late for anyone to interfere.

In spite of the early hour, the streets leading into the Bowl and its parking lot were full as they approached. Of course the limo didn't have to wait but moved smoothly to the front of the line to discharge Cleo and her unwanted entourage at the backstage entrance. She caught a number of stares in her direction, most of them hostile, some merely curious, but no one looked likely to be helpful.

With all the publicity over the event—the destruction of a real, live vampire—she'd hoped that some of the parafolk might have shown up, but that appeared to be too much to hope for. Well, she could hardly blame them. She'd done nothing to make herself welcome, spending more of her energy running away than trying to make herself part of their society.

Cleo resisted the urge to sigh aloud. No last-minute wave of nightwalkers, spellcasters or shapeshifters was riding to her rescue. It looked like she was as good as toast.

Literally.

The mind-shielded heavies escorting her kept a good grasp on her arms as they made their way backstage to where a large wooden chair waited. They sat her there and fastened her chains to the arms, securing her.

Cleo's internal clock told her that it was about an hour before dawn. The pre-show on stage was in full swing. A choir was singing something extremely religious but catchy. Cleo found herself humming along with it, to the confusion of her guards, who she now decided to nickname T-Dumb and T-Dumber.

"Doesn't that music bother you?" asked T-Dumb, who was blond, broad-shouldered and stupid-looking. T-Dumber could have been his twin brother but for the darker shade of his hair.

The choir finished the verse and began the chorus again. Rather than answering the question, Cleo sang along, reciting the lyrics exalting God on high. Both men's eyebrows went up and Cleo couldn't resist smiling. She'd briefly trained for the musicals that were so popular in the twenties and thirties, but her conversion and immediate retirement from the movie business—and life, she thought sadly—had interfered with her performing. Her voice was good...not great, but she had a nice tone, solid range and quite a bit of power when she wanted. It was fun to see their looks of surprise that she could sing.

But then she realized that they were mostly surprised that lightning didn't strike her dead for singing a religious song and she grew depressed again. Her sadness grew and she felt the first mist of tears in her eyes.

Cleo sniffed aloud. "Surely you don't believe that I'm so evil that God would smite me just for singing about him." She folded her arms and glared at them. "I'll have you know I've never done anything wrong in my life. I've never hurt anyone, certainly never killed anyone. Can you say that?"

T-Dumb and T-Dumber gave each other wary glances then shrugged. "Everyone knows that vampires are evil," T-Dumber said.

"Everyone is wrong. I'm not evil...not even close to evil. Besides, I'm not a vampire," she added quickly but they simply turned away from her. Tears welled in her eyes and she let out a sob. "I'm not a vampire."

"If you aren't then the sun won't hurt you, will it?" one of them said. She thought it was T-Dumber, but with her vision blurred she couldn't tell for certain. "If nothing happens to you then we'll let you go."

Cleo couldn't help the tears now freely running down her face, most likely ruining her mascara, but she wasn't worried about that anymore. No one she cared about would see her anyway, and she was going to die soon.

"I'm allergic to the sun. It makes me blotchy," she wailed.

Like most men, her guards weren't used to dealing with a crying woman and both now appeared distinctly uncomfortable. "Yeah, but unless you're a vampire it won't kill you. So just relax." They exchanged troubled looks.

T-Dumb spoke. "You're going to spoil your makeup. You don't want to look a mess when you go out on stage."

She continued to cry and rubbed her hands across her face, smearing what was left of her carefully applied blush. "They aren't going to let me go. No one will. Even if I don't die, they'll kill me anyway."

Both T-men crossed their arms and looked fierce. "Not with us around. If you aren't what they say you are, we'll make sure you go free," T-Dumber said. "Don't you worry about that."

Well, at least they were on her side...if she didn't die. Not that she could survive exposure to the sun, but maybe somehow she could convince them she wasn't a vampire before then. One of the men disappeared and returned with a handful of tissues. Cleo blotted her eyes but nearly cried again at the black smear on the tissues.

She looked helplessly at her now much friendlier guards. "Look what I've done to my face! I can't go out like this...could you find someone to help?"

The dark-haired T-man disappeared and soon a woman appeared carrying a large tackle box that opened to reveal makeup supplies. "I'm Beth," she announced then clucking softly she repaired the damage to Cleo's face with professional zeal.

From the stage Cleo heard the choir finish their last angelic song, then an announcer introduced Phinious Jones to the cheering mob in the stadium. Her hands became fists as the first oily phrases of her nemesis rolled out of the loudspeakers. She couldn't make out all of the words, but she knew he was talking about her.

The makeup woman, Beth, finished her job and patted Cleo on the knee. "Okay, that's done. I used waterproof mascara but try not to cry anymore. It will make your eyes puffy."

The T-men looked frankly admiring. "Nice job! I'd scarcely recognize her under all that goop," said T-Dumb, T-Dumber nodding in fervent agreement.

"You look like a new woman," he said.

"They're going to kill me," Cleo whispered, trying her most pathetic look on Beth. Who knew, maybe she'd do something to help.

The other woman merely put her brushes away, but before she left, gave a short squeeze on Cleo's shoulder, looked around carefully then stared into Cleo's eyes.

In her mind a mental voice, distinctly feminine, spoke a single word. *Courage.*

Then Beth hurried away, leaving Cleo to stare after her, astonishment mixing with new hope. Maybe she wasn't as alone as she thought she was.

Chapter Thirteen

ॐ

Cleo was still wondering over the makeup woman and her mental message when Phinious ended his speech. From the speakers on stage came her own voice, reciting lines she'd recorded seventy-plus years before. They must have started the film retrospective, Cleo decided.

For a moment Cleo wished she could see it herself. It sounded like they'd picked some of her better films, not the real cheesy ones. Even *Bride of the Monster* was excerpted and it was her best scene from the movie. At least the Watchers had good taste.

The film clips ended and Phinious returned to the microphone. In the sudden silence of the crowd Cleo had no trouble making out his words.

"So, that's what she was like then, a two-bit actress who never did anything of importance. Would you like to see what she looks like now, a nearly hundred-year-old woman?"

There was cheering and then a rhythmic chant began among the Hollywood Bowl's audience, echoing around the hills behind the seats and entering the stage's shell. Easily she made out the words: "Lutz, Lutz, Lutz…"

They were calling for her to come on stage. Cleo swallowed and tried to control her fear as the T-men unfastened the chains holding her to the bench and helped her to her feet. With gentle but firm pressure, they pushed her down a long dark corridor toward the brightly lit stage beyond. As they reached the opening Cleo hesitated but then she used her nightwalker strength to shake off the firm hands of her keepers and they stepped away, astonished that she was able to free herself from them.

She straightened her shoulders and the fall of her dress and even shook out the kinks in her chains. Phinious' last words had fired her pride as nothing else could. She was a movie star, damn it—not just a two-bit actress—and she was about to act the part of her lifetime. Head up, she stepped boldly into the lights illuminating the still pre-dawn stage. From the corner of her eye she saw the video cameras capturing her every move to project onto the screens behind her, and there was the flash of hundreds of bulbs taking her picture. She almost smiled for them but instead schooled her expression into one of complete disdain.

If she was going to die, let her at least do it with dignity. She considered giving them a speech but decided to let her actions speak for her.

From the crowd came a few jeers but as she stood firm they grew silent. She moved forward, her escort right behind her. In the far front of the stage stood a single post, placed out of the shadow of the concrete shell, where the sun would hit once it rose. That had to be where they intended her to wait for her big moment of immolation. For an instant her resolve was shaken, but then she stepped toward it as if it held no fear for her.

She could feel the approval of her guards at her boldness and remembered their promise to free her if she survived the sunrise. More and more they believed she wasn't an evil vampire.

Too bad she was. A vampire that is, not evil. A bit naughty sometimes, but not all bad. Unfortunately, it was her being a vampire that would kill her. If being evil were enough to cause someone's death by sunlight then Phinious would scarcely have been able to survive in the sun.

As they fastened her to the post, she tried to relax against it. An odd thought came to her. This wasn't nearly as fun as the last time she'd been chained to something, when she and Michael had acted out the scene with Lord Havamore and Lady Alison. Now that had been fun. In spite of Cleo's fear, a trickle of desire sped through her, just remembering Michael making love to her against the wall.

They'd caught all that on film…would Michael ever watch it? She hoped he remembered the way she looked then and not the way she would be shortly, her skin black and burned.

She'd always fallen asleep as soon as the sun came up and she hoped being in the sunlight didn't change that. At least there wouldn't be any pain involved, she hoped. That was one reason some nightwalkers sat in the sun to end their lives, Michael had told her, that it was said to be painless.

It was nearly dawn now. She could feel it in her bones, in the prickling of her skin and the way her muscles sagged in the growing light. It was the same sensation she'd felt every morning for more than seventy years…it seemed strange to realize it would be her last.

She gasped as the hillside in front of her brightened and the sky lightened to a near perfect blue. Beautiful, she couldn't help thinking and she smiled. She'd forgotten how beautiful a morning sky could be. No wonder Michael hadn't wished to give it up.

It was a perfect last image to take with her to eternity, the brightening sky and the green hillside beneath it. If only the movie would end here, cut and fade to black so she wouldn't have to live through the next few moments. But it didn't end and instead the blue sky became the color of Michael's mind.

Michael…another last thought for him, her lover now lost forever. *Goodbye, my love.*

The scene was now too bright for her eyes but she couldn't keep them open anyway. Cleo closed them and sagged in her chains against the post, barely conscious of her surroundings. The sun must be over the shell behind her.

The prickling intensified as if her skin was on fire and she nearly broke her silence to cry out at the pain. So much for passing out first! The pain was too intense for her to peacefully fall asleep.

A flash of light surrounded her, blinding her even through her closed eyelids, and Cleo flinched at the glare. In that instant she heard the faint sound of machinery and the clink of silver chains, and for a brief moment she felt like she was falling.

Then it was quiet and dark, and while she was still attached to the post, her skin no longer burned. The chains holding her to the post parted and then cool arms enclosed her, cooler than her skin, still smoldering from her exposure to the sun.

Cool and familiar arms. Barely believing it possible, Cleo fell back into those ever-so-familiar arms that lifted to hold her against an equally familiar chest. She breathed in deeply of Michael's signature scent.

Voices impinged on her bare awareness, men's voices concerned and angry.

"Is she all right?" a concerned one questioned.

"She will be." That was Michael's voice and she could feel his anger. "That was far too close though."

While apologetic, the other man's voice turned adamant. "I know, but we had to wait until the last moment, when the sun would be in everyone's eyes, or the swap wouldn't work. The timing had to be just right."

Cleo couldn't resist speaking to him, although she was too close to unconsciousness to talk aloud. She reached for

Michael with her mind and found his morning sky blueness open to her. *You came for me...rescued me...I didn't think you would.*

In her mind came his mental voice and if possible it sounded even angrier. *Of course I did...we did...I said you would always have my protection...* His thoughts sputtered to a halt. He held her closer and she felt him tremble, the strain as he controlled himself. She heard his inner struggle and the way he berated himself for her near miss.

Not your fault, Michael. Thank you for coming.

She wasn't sure if he believed her but when he bespoke her again, he sounded less agitated. *Rest now, Cleo. You are safe. We'll talk in the evening.*

Chapter Fourteen

Cleo awoke to peaceful darkness and a feeling of well-being she hadn't experienced in...well, nearly a week. She hadn't felt like this since she'd left Michael and fallen into the hands of the Paranormal Watchers.

She felt comfortable. Safe. Fed.

Fed? Cleo sat up in what she now realized was a large bed in a room she didn't recognize at all. Rich, heavily carved antique furniture took up much of the space, and heavy metal shutters similar to those at the beach house sealed the room's several windows...obviously a place set up for a nightwalker's safe daytime sleep, with no chance of sunlight entering.

That reminded her of her burns from her brief exposure to the sun and the sores she'd gotten from the silver chains. A quick inspection of her arms and ankles showed no sign of either. The skin was as smooth and perfect as always. Somehow she'd been healed.

In her mouth was the lingering taste of blood as if she'd been force-fed while she slept. Someone had fed her, a companion with healing blood, no doubt, since her sores were gone. But not Michael. She would have known his taste and this was that of a stranger.

Well, of course it wasn't Michael's blood, she realized. Michael wasn't a companion anymore—thanks to her. After a week without the marks he probably wasn't able to heal her anymore, so he must have asked someone else to feed her. Perhaps they even kept a certain amount of companion blood around for emergencies, in little plastic bags in a refrigerator.

In her unconscious state all they'd have to do is make her swallow.

Even so she knew he'd been there. Michael couldn't have fed her, but she knew that he'd been the one in her unconscious mind, helping her to drink the blood she needed, even if it hadn't been his own.

Abruptly she realized that was one of the main reasons she felt so good. Even after everything she'd done to him, Michael had rescued her and had been the one to carry her to safety this morning when she'd been helpless. More than that, she could see that the pillow next to her was dimpled as if someone else had shared the bed with her, protecting her in her daytime sleep. She leaned over and took a deep whiff of the pillowcase, taking in his distinctive smell.

It seemed Michael still wanted her, in spite of everything.

Unaccustomed tears rose in her eyes. The second time she'd cried in less than twenty-four hours, but at least these were tears of joy. She cleaned them off her face with the pillowcase, happy that someone had also thought to remove her makeup so that she didn't leave it a mess.

Abruptly, Cleo pulled herself out of bed. Having woken up wearing nothing more than her underwear, Cleo looked around for clothes. On a nearby chair she found not only the white gown she'd worn to her execution but a folded pair of comfortable-looking jeans and a sweatshirt from the state university.

Cleo couldn't help laughing when she shook it out and examined it. Someone had taken the bear logo and added a set of wicked-looking vampire fangs to the otherwise cuddly emblem. Obviously one of her hosts had a mischievous sense of humor. Under the chair was a pair of sneakers in her size to complete the outfit—much more comfortable than the silver-colored sandals she'd worn last night.

Dressing quickly, Cleo hesitated a moment before exiting the bedroom's closed door. From the understated elegance of her surroundings, these weren't just any parafolk she was about to meet, but someone of significance. Probably someone who'd been involved in her rescue and from what she remembered about that the planning for it must have been pretty elaborate.

Another thing. She bet Michael was somewhere close as well. It was time to face him and the others. She took a deep breath and let it out slowly, finding her inner calm. She was Cleo Lutz, former movie star. At one time she'd even done her own stunts. What was facing a roomful of parafolk compared to coping with a psychotically reckless director while dangling from a moving train?

Cleo took a moment to shudder at that memory. Good thing her leading man had kept a good grip on her or she never would have lived long enough to become a hundred-year-old nightwalker.

Okay, so she was only ninety-nine, but she almost hadn't made it to the century mark and the reason she would was outside this room. Squaring her shoulders, she opened the door.

The hallway was like the bedroom she'd come from, dark red carpet, tasteful oil paintings that were likely originals and more rich furniture. From around a corner she heard music and conversation and that led her to a large room filled with people, laughing and talking.

All were dressed as casually as she was, several wearing sweatshirts and jeans in spite of the obvious elegance of their surroundings, so at least as far as that was concerned Cleo was immediately put at ease.

They didn't notice her entrance as all eyes were glued to a big-screen television displaying what Cleo recognized as a recording of the Hollywood Bowl show from that morning.

Phinious was speaking with the sound turned down, and various people were providing rudely hilarious dialogue for him, hence the jeers and laughter from the crowd. Cleo found herself laughing aloud with them.

On a nearby table she saw food and drinks laid out, including various liquors and a large carafe on ice containing a straw-colored liquid that, from the color and smell, she identified as serum. She helped herself to a glass and then after a moment's consideration added a healthy dose of vodka to it. She'd had a few hard days and an even harder morning and had wandered into a party. A drink was just what she needed before finding Michael.

She heard his laughter over the sound of the others' and opened her mind to hear him better. As soon as her internal ear was open, she realized how many other mental voices there were in the room. Well over half of those present must have had psychic powers. It was almost like a completely separate conversation was taking place.

So this was a gathering of the parafolk, the people that Michael had wanted her to meet and join. They didn't look all that different from normal people.

Some seemed to spend less time talking aloud, obviously speaking with their inner voices instead, probably spellcasters, while others displayed considerably heavier body and facial hair than she would normally expect to see. She was surprised to see Beth, the makeup woman who'd spoken with her that morning, with a glass of red wine in her hand, chatting with Horace, the weak norm who'd wanted to become a nightwalker...or so he'd said.

Now she heard his real mental voice, strong and powerful, and knew he'd deliberately deceived her so she would feed from him.

Cleo laughed into her vodka and serum. So there had been parafolk hidden among the Watchers. As alone as she'd felt while being held, help had been around her all the time.

No one had noticed her yet, and she was just wondering if she wanted to keep it that way when Phinious' speech ended and the film clips of her movie career began. There was a call for silence and the sound was turned up. Cleo watched amazed as everyone in the room sat spellbound by the series of clips of her old movies. The Watchers had done a wonderful job of singling out some of her best moments.

"She was really good," came one harsh whisper after a particularly poignant scene. A young man who looked remarkably hair-free even for a norm seemed to be wiping tears from his eyes and it made Cleo smile that he'd been so affected by her performance.

"She still is, Kurt," another whispered back, and this time Cleo recognized the young werewolf, Tammy, who'd helped Michael at the studio. "Mike's got some new footage of her that is terrific."

"Really? What's he going to do with it?"

"He was talking about a new studio where our kind could work."

"Cool!" Kurt's enthusiasm was palpable and the pair continued to discuss the matter, their voices growing louder until several people shushed them.

Michael was right, Cleo realized with excitement. There really was interest among the parafolk in making movies.

"Here she comes!" someone from the front of the room cried and everyone's attention was suddenly riveted to the screen. Cleo saw her recorded self enter the Hollywood Bowl's stage and was pleased to see no sign of the fear that she knew had gripped her. Instead she stood tall and straight, head high, her calm expression as regal as any queen's. The camera centered on her face and Cleo noted that Beth's makeup job looked terrific, far better than what she'd been able to accomplish.

Her former guards, the T-men, followed her to the stake and fastened her securely, stepping back but keeping a firm watch over her and the crowd nearby. Curious as to how she'd been freed, Cleo crept close enough to hear Michael talking quietly to a tall dark-haired gentleman.

"Shouldn't Ms. Lutz be here?" the other man said. Cleo noted his accent, vaguely European but with long practice of speaking English in America.

Cleo watched Michael hesitate then shrug. "She was so tired she slept past sunset. I didn't want to wake her."

She had, Cleo realized with a start. For the first time in as long as she could remember, she'd missed awakening as soon as the sun had left the sky.

Michael was still talking. "She's been through so much. I think she may need a day or so to recover. I don't want her pushing herself."

The other man chuckled and Cleo could now see the sharp fangs in his mouth. "I think you have fallen in love, my friend. Not that I blame you, she is gorgeous."

"More so than I am?" A slender woman with hair like pale sunshine flowing down her back took his arm. From her amused expression Cleo could see she wasn't truly concerned but was teasing the nightwalker.

Even so he was quick to pull her close into his arms. "No one is as lovely as you, *meine süsse*." He nuzzled the side of her face, his fingers tracing twin scars on her neck. "No woman could be more than my bloodmate is to me."

Cleo watched the pair, obviously very much in love. This woman was more than just a matter of a healthy snack. They were as close as any human couple could be, with the added advantage of years ahead of them to enjoy that closeness.

What she wouldn't give to have someone like that to share the long years with. Cleo stole a glance at Michael and was stunned to see the look of raw envy on his face. That's what he wanted too...to be as close as this nightwalker was to his bloodmate. He had wanted that with her. Maybe still did.

She watched his jaw tighten as the recording of her near death at the Hollywood Bowl continued, the sky lightening as the sun rose in the sky behind the bowl. When the first light hit her chained body, Cleo flinched at the remembered pain, but Michael clenched his fists and looked enraged. Cleo focused on the image on the screen. In just moments would come her rescue...

And there it was. There was a flash, bright enough to make her cover her eyes. She opened them, expecting to see the stake empty. But she still stood there — or at least someone who looked very much like her, dressed in the same gown and silvery sandals, still held by silver chains to the post in the middle of the stage and looking completely unaffected by the sunlight pouring over her. Cleo's jaw dropped open. How had they managed this?

Now completely illuminated by the rising sun, her recorded image stared at the astonished crowd around her, rattled her silver chains and cried out loudly, "I am not a vampire!"

Pandemonium broke out on the stage. True to their word to free her if she survived the sunrise, the T-men rushed forward and broke open the locks that held her to the stake. Once her hands were free, Cleo's double jerked on her upper teeth, dislodging what were apparently caps and revealing an even smile.

She pointed to Phinious and the other members of the Watchers' Society on the stage. "These men have made fools of you. They lured you here and took your money, promising to show you the death of a real vampire. But I'm still alive because there are no such things, any more than there are werewolves or other paranormal folks worth watching."

In the living room the parafolk crowd cheered as the Watchers' audience went crazy, some of them storming the stage. Cleo watched the T-men hurry her double away from the crowd, although they didn't seem nearly as interested in her as they were in the Watchers. Soon the camera showed nothing but chaos as the Hollywood Bowl audience demonstrated their anger over what they saw as a phony exhibition. Phinious and his cronies took flight, although the Watchers' leader screeched as he left that they'd been set up and that a trick had been played on them.

In the room around her the parafolk laughed. "You've got that right," hooted one.

The dark-haired nightwalker stepped onto a raised platform in the corner of the room and held up his hands. "My friends, this is an evening of celebration…once again we've embarrassed and foiled the efforts of our self-proclaimed enemies, the Paranormal Watchers Society, and in the bargain rescued a member of our society…or at least someone we would like to claim that way."

Cleo felt a mental brush against her mind, like the touch of a gentle hand. There was age in that touch…she looked up to see the dark-haired nightwalker looking straight at her.

I am Jonathan Knottman, Ms. Lutz, Parafolk Chief of Los Angeles. This gathering is in part in your honor and I would like to announce your presence. Do you mind if I do?

The soft elegance of his question made her smile. Here was an old one for certain, a nightwalker with long years behind him. She nodded as she gave him a mental answer. *I would be honored.*

He smiled, fangs flashing, and she felt his welcome. Here was someone she could learn much from, and not just how to keep a companion happy. Jonathan Knottman was someone who deserved her respect.

"I know you are all concerned about our guest of honor and the injuries she sustained, so I am happy to say that she has recovered enough to be with us tonight." He held out his hand to her. "If you will join me here, Ms. Lutz?"

Distinctly conscious of every eye upon her, including those of a startled Michael Brown, Cleo made her way to Jonathan's platform. As she went, people smiled and patted her on the back until she felt more than welcome.

Why had she ever doubted her acceptance among these people? They didn't know her but they liked her anyway. It was like it had been with Michael, or the shapeshifters who'd helped him at the studio. The thought hit her so suddenly that she stood still.

She wasn't an aberration in their view, not a monster or anything like that. She was one of them. For the first time in as long as she could remember, Cleo wasn't alone. She had a community. A society, as Jonathan had put it.

She wasn't alone.

Cleo smiled and then that wasn't enough. She cried, tears running from her eyes as they had before. She was safe and comforted and with people like herself. It was a great feeling.

Only one thing remained to make it complete. The love of a wonderful man. She met Michael's intense stare and nodded to him. He didn't completely thaw towards her—she still felt some of the reserve from this morning in him—but he smiled at her just a little and that was a start.

"Thank you all for your warm welcome," she told them when they'd finished applauding. "And thanks also for my rescue...although I'm still a little mystified as to how that was accomplished. Who was that woman playing me at the end?"

"That would be me." A slender woman with brown hair stood up, a mischievous grin on her face. "With false fangs, a wig and a lot of makeup." She glanced sheepishly at Cleo. "It isn't easy playing someone like you."

"The stake was put over a trapdoor on the stage with an identical stake beneath," a man who introduced himself as Andrew explained, and Cleo recognized him as the man who'd been with Michael under the stage that morning. "Both you and Gabriella here were dressed the same and made up the same, thanks to Beth the makeup artist. When the sun was in most people's eyes, we caused a bright flash at the pole's base, and while everyone's eyes were blinded, including the camera lenses, we swapped poles. You disappeared and Gabriella appeared within the second. No one could tell she wasn't you."

Stunned, Cleo stared at Gabriella. "You took a big risk, replacing me. Suppose they'd killed you in my place?"

"We had people in the crowd whose job it was to get me out of there, but it turned out not to be necessary. You already had that handled," Gabriella said with a laugh. "It was a stroke of genius to get those guards to agree to protect you if you weren't burned by the sun. That promise really saved me some trouble getting out of there. With those two I couldn't have been safer once they realized I wasn't a nightwalker. I was out of there, in the limo and halfway to the beach before any of the Watchers had a chance to do anything." She grasped Cleo's hand and shook it firmly. "Brilliant thinking to save my butt."

"I'm glad they helped," Cleo said, still a little overwhelmed. "But I wasn't thinking of you at the time. I didn't know you'd be there."

A silence spread over the room and Gabriella stared at her. "You didn't know we'd be there? You mean you walked out on that stage expecting to die?" She turned to Michael, who stood staring at Cleo. "Didn't you tell her our plan?"

He opened his mouth, closed it then opened it again. "I couldn't," he said finally, his eyes miserable. "There isn't a bond between us. I couldn't reach her without alerting them."

"No bond? But you're her companion."

Jonathan held up his hands. "It took great courage for Ms. Lutz to face them. Cleopatra, you have our respect for your courage and dignity." He applauded and everyone joined in, even Michael, but then he turned and left the room. Cleo started to follow him but Jonathan put his hand on her arm, restraining her.

Let him go. There is much we need to discuss.

Reluctantly, Cleo gave in to the senior nightwalker's authority. Jonathan spoke for a little longer about the lesson taught the Watchers then excused himself and Cleo, encouraging everyone to enjoy the party. The blonde lady he'd spoken to earlier came to the miniature stage with a guitar and began to sing as Jonathan led Cleo through the crowd.

He stopped at the doorway to the hall and listened for a moment with a smile of sheer delight on his face. Cleo saw the love in Jonathan's eyes.

"She sings beautifully," she said, keeping her voice quiet.

"Yes, she does. Her name is Sharon Colson." Cleo recognized the name as that of one of LA's top musical performers. Jonathan nodded. "An exceptional woman in all ways. Some would say she's the other part of my soul as well as my bloodmate. I would not disagree."

He led her to a comfortable office with leather furniture and more antique wood. From a small refrigerator he pulled a pitcher of serum and a bottle of vodka. "Would you like me to freshen your drink?"

She put her nearly forgotten half-filled glass on the table. "No thank you. I think I may need a clear head."

Jonathan smiled. "A wise woman." He replaced the items and took a seat in a large wing chair, beckoning her to take the matching one opposite. Steepling his fingers, he stared over them at her for a moment. Cleo felt the weight of that measuring stare but sat impassive until he finally nodded his head.

"It is good to meet you at last. There had been rumors of Rodriquez doing unauthorized conversions, but we could never prove anything. He must have kept you well hidden to avoid our notice."

"He told me that he was the only vampire in Los Angeles. He also told me to stay out of sight and that we were in danger at all times."

Jonathan nodded. "On your own you would be. Michael explained much about your situation when he came to us after your capture. He needed help for your rescue."

"He told you what I did to him?"

"Not in so many words. I would like to hear the story from you."

She glossed over how Michael had held her captive in the studio but told him about using the soundstage for making movies. She also told him how she'd inadvertently marked him and then how she'd later removed the marks. "I didn't want a companion," she said finally. "At least not a mortal one. I was afraid to see him grow old and die."

"He told you that companions live extra-long lives and that bloodmates have nearly the immortality of a nightwalker?"

"Yes, he told me." She put her hands in front of her. "But I thought it would be better if he converted."

A slow nod was Jonathan's response. "This must all be so new to you. You've lived in isolation for so many years, then all at once you have our impetuous Michael pursuing you—and he can be very determined while in pursuit of what he wants."

A slight smile stole over the nightwalker's face. "He wasn't there when you woke this evening, was he?"

"No."

"You should probably ask him where he went. I think there is much to get straightened out between you. I will say this. I am chief of the parafolk here in Los Angeles and one of my duties is to approve conversions."

"Oh?" Cleo blushed. She hadn't realized she would need to get anyone's permission or that she'd be breaking parafolk law without it. Not that she needed permission at this point, since Michael had already rejected that option.

"Have you done one before?"

"What?"

"A conversion. Have you done a conversion before?"

"No…"

Jonathan leaned forward. "The procedure is not that difficult, but you do need to take a considerable amount of blood. For that reason you can't really convert a companion. Fortunately Michael no longer has that issue since the marks were removed a week ago. You shouldn't have too much of a problem. Then you just need to feed him some of your blood. It will take overnight to finish and will be painful, as I'm sure you remember, but the process should be complete by tomorrow's rising. I'd like you to stay here in the mansion so we may be of assistance if needed."

Cleo shook her head in bewilderment. "I don't know what you are talking about."

Both Jonathan's eyebrows went up. "I'm talking about Michael's conversion. He told me you offered to make him one of us and he asked for permission on your behalf."

"But Michael refused to even consider becoming a nightwalker."

Jonathan shrugged. "I think he changed his mind. Or had it changed for him. As I said, he can be relentless when he wants something and he wants you very much. He's in love with you."

"Michael wants to become a nightwalker?"

Jonathan's smile was small. "I didn't say that—I said he loved you and wants to be with you any way you will let him. It now becomes your choice as to how that happens. There is a garden on the roof, Ms. Lutz, that is pretty overgrown but Michael likes it anyway. I suspect you will find him there."

Confusion and the need to understand made her bold. "I would like to ask you a question." She hesitated. "A personal question."

Again his eyebrows arched neatly. "If it is a personal question, then perhaps we should drop formalities between us. May I call you Cleopatra?"

"Or Cleo. That's what my friends call me...when I had friends," she amended. It had been many, many years since the last of her normal friends had died.

"You have friends again, Cleo. I would be happy if you called me Jon. So what is this 'personal question'?"

"Your companion...would you rather she was like yourself?"

He seemed to think for a moment before answering. "If that's what she wanted I would accept it. Happy couples exist where both parties are nightwalkers. But I enjoy Sharon's differences as much as she enjoys mine. For me she is all I need physically and emotionally. I drink from her and never want. That is a wonderful thing."

"She wouldn't want to be converted."

Leaning back into the chair, he shook his head. "No, she would not. My Sharon belongs to the sunlight even if she rarely spends much time there. I am glad she's chosen to share the dark with me, but I would never ask her to confine herself to my world."

Cleo thought hard. "There is a great deal I still need to know, Jon."

He smiled, his fangs showing sharp against his lower lip. "Ask your questions, Cleo. We have plenty of time."

Chapter Fifteen

ဆာ

It was much later when she found Michael on the rooftop. The place was as the nightwalker chief had described, a near jungle of a garden, and she had to explore the place for a while before finding him. Lush plantings in containers surrounded sets of tables and chairs, and in a secluded place overlooking the distant ocean was a set of two recliners.

Michael lounged in one, an open bottle of beer in his hand. He barely acknowledged her when she sat on the other. Instead he took a long pull from his bottle and watched the moonlit sea far away.

Cleo watched as well. She could feel he was in an odd mood, wanting but afraid to admit it. He wanted her to make the first move, but she knew she had to wait him out. Otherwise he would not feel as if he had any control at all.

After she made no attempt to talk to him, he finally turned to her. "Cleo—are you all right? No lasting affects?"

"I'm fine. Nothing wrong that a good feeding wouldn't help." She was hungry, she realized as her stomach growled. Michael's rich scent attracted her, making her want what flowed in his veins. But she wanted more than that.

Michael's beer bottle suddenly seemed to hold a special interest for him. He stared at it, gently loosening the label. "Hmm…a good feeding." He laughed shortly. "Well, I guess I can at least promise you that tonight." His mood changed and he grew serious again. "Cleo…you understand why I couldn't contact you at the theatre."

"You said it was because the bond was broken."

"That was part of it. Even with my psychic powers I would have had to really reach to find you, and I'm the only one who knows you well enough to find your mind. We know that the Watchers have some parafolk on staff... Traitors." He said the word bitterly. "That's how they knew to watch my house in Malibu. They would have surely had someone 'listening' for the kind of broadband call I'd have to make. We needed the element of surprise so we couldn't warn you."

She'd thought it had been something like that. "If we were still linked..."

"I could have safely reached you." He swallowed convulsively. "I just want you to know that I'm sorry I couldn't. You must have been terrified seeing the sky light up."

"It was beautiful," she said quietly. "I'd forgotten how blue the sky could be." She lay back on the recliner and watched the dark starry sky overhead. "You spent the day in bed with me but left early. Why? Where did you go?"

"I came here. I...I wanted to watch the sunset."

As she'd suspected. "You wanted to see it one more time?"

Michael put his bottle down on the nearby table on top of the peeled-off label. "Did Jonathan talk to you?"

"Yes, we talked. He told me that you talked to him too."

He hesitated. "Do you understand why?"

"I had asked you to become a nightwalker and you knew I needed permission. You asked him to give me permission to convert you."

"And?"

"And yes. I know what to do." She did too. "Is this your choice, Michael?"

Many emotions passed over his face. Traces of anxiety and pain followed by resolution. It broke Cleo's heart to see that look.

Michael seemed to stifle a sigh. "Yes. It is my choice to be converted. We should go to our room. Jonathan wants it done here just in case there are problems."

He started to rise, but Cleo didn't move from her seat. "Have you ever made love on a rooftop under the stars, Michael?" she asked dreamily.

"Not that I can remember. But this isn't the place for a — a conversion." He stuttered over the word.

Taking in his long lean form with pleasure, Cleo pitched her voice at its deepest and most sultry level. "No reason we can't make love first, Michael, is there? Up here where we're alone."

He glanced over in the direction of the door she'd used. "There's a party going on downstairs. Someone might come up here."

Cleo shrugged. "Are you worried someone might see us making love? You took all that video footage of us doing exactly that. Anyway the danger adds a little spice, don't you think?"

When he didn't protest further, she knew she had him. Cleo moved to his lounge, sitting on the edge next to him, and let her hands play across his chest. He seemed calm but his brown eyes were dark with suppressed emotions.

"What are you up to, Cleo? It seems like every time you seduce me I end up regretting it."

"You won't regret it this time, darling," she purred.

Michael caught her hands and tugged her on top of him, holding her with a firm grasp. His expression was fierce, all of his frustrations with her coming out at last. "Cleo, do you know how much I love you?

"I think I do. I think you love me as much as I do you."

"You think so?" he whispered. "Then prove it."

No words were going to win this argument. Cleo closed the gap between them and covered his mouth with hers in a kiss that completed and ended the discussion. She put everything she wanted into that kiss, opening her mind to him to show him how much she cared, how much it had meant to her that he'd come to rescue her, how sorry she was for having run away from him time after time.

Michael responded, at first tentatively, but then he grew bolder. His mind gleamed with the depths of his feelings for her, forgiving her for everything she'd done to him, grateful that she was once again with him. He loved her, pure and simple, and was willing to do anything for her.

Anything. Even give up the sun, the daylight hours, the taste of food and all else that he cared for. Everything he was he would give up to be with her.

How could she care any less for him?

She pulled away and stroked his face. He didn't want to lose her mouth—he tried to pull her back, but for once she used her strength to stop him. Instead she kissed his cheek then let her tongue slide down his neck. He tasted wonderful, rich, and she could feel the strong beat of his pulse under her tongue.

There, that was the place. Where the skin was thinnest over the vein. Cleo bit deeply into Michael's neck, holding him firm against the lounge. Her mind sought his, completely open to her, and clouded it, taking the pain before he even knew what was happening. She drank deep, sharing her joy in his blood with him. An involuntary moan passed his lips.

How could she ever have thought she could live without this man? Rich flavor filled her mouth, his human essence. Even though she'd obviously had another companion's blood earlier, healing the injuries she'd taken, even though technically he was no longer a companion, she felt wonderful after just a few sips of him. In her heart she knew the truth.

Michael was the perfect nightwalker companion — it was what he'd been born to be and it was all he wanted to be, despite his words.

Jon had given her explicit instructions. She had to drink deeply but carefully. The first stutter in his pulse told her she'd taken enough. Cleo pulled back and with a quick lick sealed the wounds — sealed but didn't remove. When she was done the marks remained in his flesh, pinpoint scars from her fangs.

Still following instructions Cleo put two fingers to cover the twin marks. "This is my choice, Michael. I choose you to be my companion, to serve me as long as you wear my mark. In exchange you have my support and protection from this time on."

The confusion in Michael's face began to clear and he stared at her in an astonishment bordering on joy. "I thought…you said…you wanted. You wanted me to convert."

"Not any longer, Michael. I want you to be my companion — if you're still willing to do that."

He reached up and gingerly touched the marks on his neck, the ones he'd told her so many times he wanted. Hesitancy crossed his face. "You said for as long as I wear your mark. How long is that likely to be?"

A sliver of guilt over the number of times she played him false ran through her. "I guess I deserve that. But Michael, I've changed. You wanted me to commit to you and I have. I love you and want to be with you — so let's say that you'll wear those marks until you ask me to take them off. And I hope that's never."

A broad grin took over his face. "Never is good. I like never. In that case, I accept."

Michael could hardly believe it. He touched the new marks on his neck and stared at the woman crouched over him. Earlier he'd made up his mind to do whatever it took to be with Cleo...even to convert if that were the only way he'd be able to stay with her. Instead he'd gotten just what he'd wanted in the first place. The woman of his dreams was in his arms and he was her companion.

Jubilation mixed with caution and he could barely breathe. "Are you certain this is what you want?"

"I'm certain." She touched his face. "I've waited a long time for you, not even knowing what I was waiting for. I should have known when we first met that it was you. I'd faded into the shadows and forgotten who I was and you brought it back to me, gave me back the woman I have to be. When I stepped onto that stage this morning I was Cleopatra Lutz again and I have you to thank for that. You made me remember who I was."

"But what about the rest, Cleo? I'm still human. It will take a long time but I'll still age and die."

"You told me once that all living beings do that and it's how you live your life that matters. I know now you were right. I want you to be my companion and live with me and love me. I love you, Michael, just as you are. I always will, no matter how long we have together."

"Live together? So where will we live?"

She smiled. "Wherever you wish, Michael. That will be your choice."

His choice. He knew where he wanted to go. "I did take the liberty of moving your bed again. To that house on the hill overlooking the ocean."

"You did? What about the studio?"

"My company just purchased the Eagan Brothers lot for Fly by Night Films but I wanted to talk to you before we went any further there."

She nodded slowly. "So, this house of yours. Is there a lightproof bedroom in it?"

"There is an excellent nightwalker bedroom in it, Cleo. I had light sensitive shutters installed—I thought I might need them."

His smile faded a little. "Cleo, thank you. For understanding why I didn't want to convert."

"No, Michael, thank you. For bringing back my memory of who I am and giving me so many new ones to cherish."

"New memories. Yes, I like the sound of that." Mischief crept into his eyes and with a sudden move he turned them so that she was now beneath him on the lounge. "And now, as my first act as your sworn companion, I insist that we make love."

Cleo couldn't help tease him. "Out here, in the open? Someone might see us."

"Anyone who wants to watch us in action can get a ticket to our first film," he grinned down at her. "Otherwise they'll have to leave."

"You aren't planning to use any of that footage from the studio!" Cleo said, suddenly concerned.

Michael broke into laughter. "Never fear. I'd never expose you that way. That footage is purely for my private Cleopatra Lutz collection."

Now Cleo laughed with him. "I imagine the way we're going that collection will eventually be even bigger than my released material."

He nuzzled her neck. "It will be if I have anything to say about it. I'll show you some of it later—it can be very inspirational. But right now I need no inspiration to make love to you."

"So let's make love."

Michael kissed her, tasting the residue of his blood in her mouth, and felt the slight ache on his neck from the marks she'd given him. The sweetness of his blood, the glorious ache of the marks — the joy of being a companion again.

This is what he'd wanted, what he'd wished in that moment in the bar when he'd spotted her. He was now her sworn companion and nothing and no one would ever stand between them again, not even themselves. He kissed her with all of his being and soul, wanting to claim her the way she'd claimed him. He was her companion — she was his nightwalker for now and for always.

Cleo knew things were different now as well. When they'd made love before she'd always held back, but no longer. Now Cleo opened to him, both her body and mind, and he could see every thought she had. Her hesitancy and confusion, the result of her experience with her maker and her long lonely years in hiding, were gone.

Michael knew from talking with Chief Jon that Rodriquez had been a rogue vampire, not respecting of any rules he didn't agree with. He'd taken Cleo against her will and turned her without a choice. She hadn't known anything but what he taught her, making her the easily spooked creature he'd found, hiding from the world and herself. She'd turned her back on everything she'd once loved to keep safe.

This Cleo was no longer afraid of anything, a remarkable fact given how close she'd come to death today. Maybe she thought she needed a protector? But no, he knew it was more than that. At last Cleo had decided to trust him, and knowing he'd earned that trust pleased him more than if she'd simply surrendered in the first place.

Rising over her, Michael lifted the vampire bear sweatshirt she wore to find her breasts, unencumbered by a bra. He feasted on them, using his tongue and lips to tease her nipples into hardened peaks while his hands explored the soft full mounds, caressing and kneading them until Cleo was moaning from the pleasure.

"Like that, Michael. Oh, yessss." She drew out the last word as he sucked hard on one coral nipple.

Her hands took to exploring his body, slipping open the buttons of his shirt to find his chest. Soft but insistent, her fingers played on his bare chest, tugging lightly on the hair around his nipples then fingering the tiny nubs, mimicking his movements. Her touch sent shock waves into his cock until he could have exploded right then, just from the touch of her fingers on his chest.

It had been over a week since he'd made love with Cleo and he wasn't going to last more than a few minutes if he didn't slow things down somehow. Coming too quickly was not the way he wanted Cleo to remember their making love this night.

No, he wanted her screaming his name as he came deep inside her, her lips on his neck, sucking sweetly. He wanted her mind joined with his, fully this time.

He wanted no barriers between them, not now. It was his right as her companion to ask that they join completely. Leaning away from her, he studied Cleo's face, bright with passion in the light from the half-moon behind him. Her eyes were wide and he could feel how puzzled she was that he'd stopped making love to her. Opening his mind, he invited her in.

At first hesitant, then bolder, Cleo took him up on that offer, pulling down the barriers between their thoughts. With the practice of sixty years of living with nightwalkers and other mentally powered beings, Michael slipped inside her mind and for the first time really saw Cleo's thoughts and who she really was.

He saw how conflicted she'd been. Trusting was hard for her…it went against all her instincts to let him see this deeply into her mind. She was a woman used to keeping her secrets.

She was a woman who'd been terribly alone for a very long time.

You aren't alone any longer, Cleo. I am your companion, now and always.

A soft joy permeated her thoughts, like a newborn smile or the first hint of dawn. Something new for her…Cleo wasn't alone and for the first time she actually believed it. She believed in him and what he offered her and she wanted it as much as he did.

With a shout Michael drew her up into his arms, no longer caring that anyone might hear them on the open rooftop. He gave her a kiss so passionate that it left both of them breathless and incapable of movement.

Then they were both in action, tearing off clothes, removing all barriers, physical and mental, from each other. Michael had to force his hands to slow down, to savor the touch of her, but savoring took too much time. He craved her too much.

This wasn't the occasion for slow and easy lovemaking…they could do that later. After all they had decades ahead to make love.

Then she was naked beneath him, all pale in the moonlight, parts of her in shadow from where he blocked the light. Cleo gazed up at him, love in her eyes and her smile. Love for him.

He touched her cheek with his hand and her mind with his and let his thoughts mingle with hers. Slowly he entered her and the sensation of his cock sliding into her warmth became a shared experience. He felt how hard he was to her as he sheathed himself completely, shared how her tight and welcoming her pussy was, their minds as joined as their bodies.

Michael had to stop and breathe deeply. This was too much. He'd never done this before, made love with such completely shared minds. Forget lasting two minutes, he wasn't going to go more than a second before coming.

Cleo's mind was pure golden flame, her emotions awhirl with their coupling but as he hesitated one thought came through loud and clear. *If you don't start moving, Michael, I'm going to...* She didn't have to finish her threat because he pulled back and thrust deeper, and he felt both her and his side of his stroke.

Now that felt way too good not to do it again! And so he did, forgetting everything about control or stamina or anything else. It was enough to be inside the woman he loved, the woman he'd love for all time. Enough to know that he and she felt the same. They moved together in concert, two people becoming one, body, mind — and soul.

When he came it was in an explosion of vibrant sparks that rivaled the best animated film from the past. Cleo shared the fireworks with him, all the colors possible in and outside the edges of his and her perception.

Sparks seemed to fly around them as if to set the world on fire and it was almost with surprise that when at last they finally came back to themselves it was to find things around them untouched by the flames.

That surprise was the last thought they shared before the melding ceased and they slid apart, but this time it wasn't as before with Cleo slipping away from him. This time her mind stayed open and close to him and she nuzzled him under his chin.

In the aftermath, they lay together on the chaise lounge in full view of the stars and moon overhead.

Michael gave a great sigh.

Still using their mental connection, a message of alarm came from Cleo. *What's wrong?*

I wish there had been a camera around, Cleo. I would like to have a recording for my personal collection so I could remember this moment forever.

She laughed, letting her fangs show for once. It occurred to Michael that finally Cleo was comfortable with who she was and that made him smile in return. *I doubt I'll have trouble remembering this, Michael, or anything else from now on. You make me want to remember everything.*

The End

Enjoy an excerpt from

ALL NIGHT INN

Copyright © JANET MILLER, 2005.

All Night Inn

"Ms. Colson." Jonathan came upon her so quietly she startled, dropping the rag. He watched silently as she recovered her composure. "You did well tonight. I have no objection to continuing your employment." He eyed the cloth on the counter then turned his intense blue stare back to her. "What are your feelings about it?"

Shaken, but not deterred. With a boldness she didn't feel, she stared back at him. "I still want the job."

Just for an instant a smile slipped across his lips. "Very well." He inclined his head, and pointed to the hallway leading to his office. "That way, please."

She preceded him inside. It wasn't a large room. Jonathan's desk took up the bulk of the space in the middle. In one corner was a brown leather couch, easily six feet long, with a colorful striped blanket spread across the back. A mini-fridge sat next to it, doubling as a lamp stand. For a moment Sharon speculated as to what kind of drinks her future boss kept cold. Little plastic bags from the local blood bank, perhaps?

Heart pounding, she eyed the couch and waited. Jonathan followed her gaze, hesitated, and apparently decided against the intimacy that would afford. He directed her toward the top of the desk with an elegant wave of his hand. "If you will sit there, Ms. Colson?"

She did as he instructed, facing him as he approached. For the first time since that brief caress in the bar, he touched her, placed his hands on her shoulders. She'd thought they'd be cold, clammy, but there was perceptible warmth to them. She felt it through the thin material of her blouse. Not warm enough to be human, but there.

For a moment he studied her face. "You're sure about this?"

Sharon closed her eyes and steeled herself for the sensation of his mouth on her throat, the prick of his teeth piercing the skin. She hated pain. She was the kind to insist on local anesthesia before allowing a splinter to be removed.

"Just do it," she whispered.

He did nothing. She opened her eyes and his blue stare bore into her. "You must look into my eyes and let me into your mind, Ms. Colson. I'll take the fear from you and make it easy."

He wanted to link minds with her? Panicked, Sharon shook her head. "No, not that. I won't let you do that."

He frowned. "You don't understand. I can block what you feel and make it pleasurable for you. Without a mind link there will be pain."

"I do understand. I expect the pain. I can deal with it."

He shook his head, displeasure infusing his expression. "I'm not in the habit of causing discomfort. I enjoy feeding..." One long finger traced the vein in her neck. "I'd rather you enjoyed it, too."

"It isn't important I enjoy it," she said, her voice desperate. How could she make him understand? Sharon took a deep and ragged breath. "There was a man I met who did a mind link to me once." She shuddered at the memory. It had been...awful. She'd felt like she'd been ripped apart and afterward...no, she couldn't think about the "afterward."

"It was months before I could think straight. I'm willing to let you feed off me, but I can't let you into my mind."

He let go of her and stepped back, disappointment in his face. "I'm very sorry, Ms. Colson. I would have enjoyed having you here...but the role of a companion requires my being able to touch your mind."

Moving to the door, he gestured to her. "Come with me to the bar, and I'll pay you for this evening."

"No!" Nervously, she licked her lips. "Please...can't you make an exception? I really need this job."

Frustration showed in his face. "Exception to what? To the mark, no, it's too dangerous for me to have unmarked humans here."

Desperation made her bold. "What about the link, then? Just this once? Maybe when I know you better, can trust you more...I promise I'll let you into my mind."

For a moment she thought he was going to give up and send her on her way. Then she caught the hungry look in his eyes and the way he studied her neck with a possessive stare. She could tell he wanted this, to taste her, to mark her as his own. He might not ever take her blood again, but he wanted it this time.

The way he licked his lips told her that he wanted it bad enough to forego his principles and bleed her without the mind link.

"As you wish, then." The vampire returned to her and took a different hold with his hands. One moved to the back of her head, the other to just below her shoulder blades. It was a more intimate embrace than the one he'd taken before—and more secure. His hand caressed her hair, pulling it back, baring her neck. It might have been the prelude to a kiss.

Piercing blue eyes stared into hers. "I will hold you to that promise," he whispered.

His arms tightened and he moved so fast that she didn't have a chance to say anything, couldn't have pulled away if she wanted to. Held in his vise-like grip, sharp pain stabbed through her as his fangs plunged into her neck, unerringly locating the artery. A burning sensation followed as strong lips drew the blood through the tiny holes.

Pain. It was worse than she'd imagined. Sharon wanted to cry out, but couldn't. He held her so close she was crushed into his chest. His throat rippled as he swallowed and she felt his heartbeat stutter then pick up pace, growing faster, almost matching the furious pounding of hers.

She hadn't expected him to take so much, just a few swallows, a taste. This was more like a banquet for him as he guzzled her life's blood. Fear grew inside her...fear of what she'd promised, of what she would become at his hands.

A vampire and companion linked minds—it was "required". How was she ever going to deal with that?

As her body chilled, his grew warmer. A rushing noise sounded in her ears and dizziness encompassed her. She grew weak and faint and still he took from her until she began to wonder if he intended to stop feeding at all, or if her life would end in his arms.

Was she going to die?

A gasp of fear and pain escaped her. Abruptly his mouth stopped moving and simply rested. He breathed heavily, the heat of his breath scorching her throat. The worst of the pain ended at the same time, but the relief from it put tears into her eyes.

His grip eased, and he allowed her to pull back, but only briefly. "A moment," he whispered. "I must stop the flow." He pressed down, covering the aching places where his teeth had pierced the skin.

She felt the touch of his tongue move across the holes, sealing them but not healing. He gently licked the rest of her neck, cleaning the remaining blood and soothing her skin. The throbbing abated under his tender ministrations.

The vampire drew back, a warm possessive glow in his eyes. An odd thought slid into her mind. *He was a neat eater.* Only the smallest amount of blood lingered at the corners of his mouth, and as she watched his flitting tongue removed even that evidence.

Deep amusement laced his voice when he spoke. "Congratulations, Ms. Colson. You have the job."

Why an electronic book?

We live in the Information Age—an exciting time in the history of human civilization, in which technology rules supreme and continues to progress in leaps and bounds every minute of every day. For a multitude of reasons, more and more avid literary fans are opting to purchase e-books instead of paper books. The question from those not yet initiated into the world of electronic reading is simply: *Why?*

1. ***Price.*** An electronic title at Ellora's Cave Publishing and Cerridwen Press runs anywhere from 40% to 75% less than the cover price of the exact same title in paperback format. Why? Basic mathematics and cost. It is less expensive to publish an e-book (no paper and printing, no warehousing and shipping) than it is to publish a paperback, so the savings are passed along to the consumer.

2. ***Space.*** Running out of room in your house for your books? That is one worry you will never have with electronic books. For a low one-time cost, you can purchase a handheld device specifically designed for e-reading. Many e-readers have large, convenient screens for viewing. Better yet, hundreds of titles can be stored within your new library—on a single microchip. There are a variety of e-readers from different manufacturers. You can also read e-books on your PC or laptop computer. (Please note that Ellora's

Cave does not endorse any specific brands. You can check our websites at www.elloras cave.com or www.cerridwenpress.com for information we make available to new consumers.)

3. *Mobility.* Because your new e-library consists of only a microchip within a small, easily transportable e-reader, your entire cache of books can be taken with you wherever you go.

4. ***Personal Viewing Preferences.*** Are the words you are currently reading too small? Too large? Too... ANNOYING? Paperback books cannot be modified according to personal preferences, but e-books can.

5. ***Instant Gratification.*** Is it the middle of the night and all the bookstores near you are closed? Are you tired of waiting days, sometimes weeks, for bookstores to ship the novels you bought? Ellora's Cave Publishing sells instantaneous downloads twenty-four hours a day, seven days a week, every day of the year. Our webstore is never closed. Our e-book delivery system is 100% automated, meaning your order is filled as soon as you pay for it.

Those are a few of the top reasons why electronic books are replacing paperbacks for many avid readers.

As always, Ellora's Cave and Cerridwen Press welcome your questions and comments. We invite you to email us at Comments@ellorascave.com or write to us directly at Ellora's Cave Publishing Inc., 1056 Home Avenue, Akron, OH 44310-3502.

Discover for yourself why readers can't get enough of the multiple award-winning publisher

Ellora's Cave.

Whether you prefer e-books or paperbacks,

be sure to visit EC on the web at

www.ellorascave.com

for an erotic reading experience that will leave you breathless.